To Michelle

No Rules

With Love & Best Wishes

Pamela Christine
x

No Rules

Pamela Christine

Copyright (C) 2019 Pamela Christine
Layout design and Copyright (C) 2019 Creativia
Published 2019 by Creativia
Edited by Jodie Robson
Cover art by Cover Mint
This book is a work of fiction. Names, characters, places, and incidents are the product of the author's imagination or are used fictitiously. Any resemblance to actual events, locales, or persons, living or dead, is purely coincidental.
All rights reserved. No part of this book may be reproduced or transmitted in any form or by any means, electronic or mechanical, including photocopying, recording, or by any information storage and retrieval system, without the author's permission.

Author Bio

Pamela Christine writes in her spare time and is based in Hull, this is her second novel. She loves to holiday in Greece and feels this is where she draws most of her inspiration from. She lives with her husband, and has a son, step daughter and three grandchildren.

Acknowledgements

I would like to start by thanking my husband for his continued support and occasional input. I would also like to thank my daughter in law Jodie for her time spent editing this book for me. Thank you to all of you who I have turned to for support and inspiration from time to time, I appreciate you being there at the end of the line. And finally, I would like to thank Andrew Wigley for his wonderful work on the front cover.

Chapter One

It's nearly six o'clock and I am running to catch the evening bus, trying to avoid falling on the icy path and stumbling all over like Bambi. 'Please wait' I beg in my thoughts. It's Friday and my car is in the local garage for repair. I have just finished my second week in a delightful school, well, compared to my last one it is.

Greenhill Comprehensive was what I would call a difficult school, with difficult children. No one can say I didn't try though, God knows I did, but after five years of disruptive children and a failed marriage I had to admit defeat and leave. Not only because of the kids, but also the fact that my ex-husband worked there.

I finally caught up with the bus and was relieved that the driver had been kind enough to wait for me. I scrambled for my change, which was at the bottom of my bag as usual, not very organised for a teacher. I made my way to the back of the bus, dragging my rucksack with me, which was full of marking that would have to be done over the weekend.

The bus was full of the usual suspects, most were pre-occupied with their mobile phones, checking social media and answering texts. I can never understand how people find it acceptable to leave the sound on their phone when they are in a public place, the last thing I want to listen to when I leave work is the shouts and screams of a "what happened next" video, and the guy next to me laughing out loud while he watches it.

My twenty-minute journey home soon came to an end, and after a short walk from the bus stop, I was home. Home, for now, was a rented place I was sharing with Caroline. Although I don't know how long for, I know she had plans to marry Jim and I'm sure they would want to find their own place together one day.

I put my key in the door, no sign of Caroline, she was probably at the gym. The last thing I would want to do when I got home would be to go to the gym, I had enough of that when I was married to Paul, who was the PE teacher back at Greenhill. There was a strong, stale smell of curry in the house that had lingered from the take away I had had the night before. Caroline had gone to a training thing from work and I couldn't be bothered to cook, which is no surprise, since I split with Paul I couldn't be bothered to do much really. All I wanted to do was get into that bath. After dropping my bag in the hallway, I kicked off my shoes and made my way upstairs, heading straight for the bathroom. I reach for my favourite bath oil from the shelf, the one Paul always used to say I hid from him and pour it liberally into the bath. I turn the taps on full before making my way into the bedroom to get undressed, then wrap my robe around me so I can quickly run downstairs to pour a glass of my favourite wine, to help me unwind completely.

I head back upstairs, grab the latest erotic novel I'm reading from my bedside table and go into the bathroom, where my bath is almost ready. Placing my wine on the lid of the wash basket at the side of the bath, I slip my robe off and let it fall to the floor in a heap. I am just easing my toe into the steaming hot water when the phone rings.

"Damn! Who could that be?" I can never leave a ringing phone, so naked I run to the bedroom. "Hello?"

"It's only me, I just wondered if you are still coming for tea on Sunday?"

"Mum" I roll my eyes at the thought of her keeping me from my bath.

"Well done Dear, yes, it's your Mum. So, are we still on for Sunday?"

"Mum I'm just getting in the bath, I'm stood naked in the bedroom"

"Well, you should have put some clothes on, or ignored the phone, it's not an emergency" She knows I can't ignore the phone. "It's just Don needs to know as his Son has asked us over and we need to know what we are doing"

Don was Mum's new friend, he seemed like a nice guy. She had met him at a salsa class a couple of years after Dad passed away, he made her happy and that's all that mattered.

"Well I don't mind either way Mum, if you want to go to Don's Son's that's fine. To be fair I have a lot of marking to do which will keep me busy. Just let me know what you are doing by lunchtime tomorrow. Now can I get my bath please?"

"Yes, of course, I'll get off and ring you tomorrow"

"Ok Mum bye"

"Bye... Oh just one more thing, did you ring Aunty Lesley about the family meal?"

"Nope. No, I didn't, I've been too busy. Anyway, I must go, I'll speak to you tomorrow, bye!" I just heard a quick bye from Mum as I put the phone down. I had to cut her off quickly or I would have been there all night.

Back in the bathroom, I quickly immersed myself in the water. I lay in the hot, bubbly water, grabbed my glass of wine and took a sip and then placed it back on the wash basket. I flicked through the pages of my book, trying to find the dog-eared corner I had turned over.

'His strong hands caressed her waiting body, exploring every inch of her olive skin. He gently kissed her breasts, sending a tingle through her spine. Enveloping her with his body she felt his manhood hard and strong.'

"Why do they call it a manhood?" I thought... anyway, I took another sip of wine and continued to read.

'As he slipped into her already wet pussy she moaned and begged him to go deeper. He pushed himself further into her, she moaned again as they rocked together to a steady rhythm.'

I could feel a bit of tingling myself. I placed my glass on the side of the bath, added some more hot water and submerged myself deep into the bath. With my book still tightly gripped in my hand I began to read the next page.

'His hands wrapped around her wrists and he stretched her arms above her head, gently licking her hard nipples. The tip of his tongue searched for her navel, tasting every inch of her smooth soft skin, she tasted so good, fresh and warm.

As he pulled away from her to move down she let out a moan, he didn't disappoint as he began exploring her waiting pussy.'

I could feel myself becoming aroused, I took another large mouthful of wine. I sunk further into the bath, my long brown hair floated in the water covering my breasts. I reached up for the shower gel, gently smothering myself in it, tenderly rubbing it over my body and slowly feeling my way around a familiar landscape. I had long abandoned my book, my fingers having already located the warmth of my clitoris beneath the water.

I rubbed rhythmically and felt a surge building up inside me, filling me with pleasure. My breasts were full and ripe, my nipples hard and erect. Closing my eyes, I began to think about Will, he was one of the sixth formers at school, naughty I know but he was over eighteen and so fit. I imagined him watching me in the bath, slowly caressing himself, moving his hands towards the crotch of his jeans, reaching for the zip and slowly unzipping it. His strong hands reaching into his pants, taking hold of and stroking his erect penis with intent, as he watched me reaching my climax.

The thought of him running his fingers through his dark hair with one hand as he gradually built up to his own orgasm filled me with delight. I could feel that I was coming. I arched my back and shuddered, a familiar numbness engulfing my body. I let out a gentle moan and was left feeling relaxed and content.

The next thing I knew Caroline was shouting upstairs, I must have fallen asleep as the bath water had gone cold.

"Lizzie?!"

"Yeah? I'm in the bath!"

"Ok, do you want a coffee?"

"Please, I'll be down in a minute"

I hurried out of the bath, popped my robe and slippers back on and made my way down to the kitchen. Caroline was already preparing our tea.

"Grilled chicken and salad ok?"

"Yes, that's fine"

Caroline was a bit of a keep fit freak, always eating healthy. And to be fair she kept me on track, I could so easily be tempted to a bar of chocolate.

"So, I'm guessing you had a takeaway last night?"

"Yes. To be honest, I was just so tired"

"It's fine, you don't need to justify yourself to me. It's your body, your choice" she said, not quite believing it herself.

'Oh, god here she goes, your body's a temple etc.' I thought.

"I'm assuming you went to the gym tonight?"

"Yeah I went straight from work"

"I don't know how you can, I'm exhausted when I leave work"

"I've told you before, it relieves my tension"

"Hmm, well I can think of better things to do to relieve my tension, that's for sure" I said, my mind wandering back to what I'd been doing in the bath half an hour ago.

"Lizzie!"

"What! Well I'm just saying"

Caroline worked in a bank and was always stressing about being under pressure to meet deadlines and targets. I didn't class it at a stressful job and there are far worse jobs out there. Take my best friend, Dawn, for instance, she worked in a call centre and had to put up with people slamming the phone down on her and being abusive, I couldn't stand that. Come to think of it, I think my job is more stressful than hers.

"So how was your day Lizzie?" Caroline asked.

"It was ok, still not met everyone yet"

"Its early days yet, you've only been there a couple of weeks. What are the kids like?"

I laughed a little. "Well, they are a lot better than at Greenhill and they're not exactly kids, more like students"

I taught the fifth year and sixth formers, most of them were ok, there was just the odd one who wasn't really interested. All in all, I couldn't complain.

We had tea and I settled down to watch the television, Caroline disappeared to her room, probably doing yoga or something. She wasn't exactly the clubbing type, she was more interested in keeping healthy, she very occasionally drank the odd glass of wine, with a meal of course, but was more into disgusting looking smoothies.

I thought about all the marking that lay ahead of me and decided to pour another glass of wine, I know it wasn't the sensible thing to do but I just couldn't face it and besides, I wasn't feeling sensible.

I thought about going to Mum's but in the end decided not to, I had way too much stuff to do, things that I had been putting off for a long time like sorting out some of the things I still had packed in boxes - and of course there was still all my marking. I rang Mum and explained that I would have to leave it this weekend, I think she was a little put out by it, but I wasn't really in the mood for small talk with Don and his family.

I didn't really want to see anyone, I wasn't good to be around at the minute. I had a lot of healing to do from my split with Paul, I was still angry and bitter over the whole thing.

Saturday was pretty much like any other Saturday. I got up around ten, scrambled myself a couple of eggs which I served on toast, and caught up with the planner on TV.

There was no sign of Caroline all day, she must have ended up sleeping out at Jim's. He was a lovely guy, very much like Caroline wanting to do everything by the book, and that's what they were doing. They had been going out for about a year now, met at college, were planning their engagement. Both were into the fitness thing and loved each other unconditionally, what more could you want?

Well, it wouldn't do for me, at least not for a long time.

Chapter Two

The weekend flew by and it was soon time for me to catch that dreaded bus again for work. My car hadn't recovered well from its MOT last week and it wasn't good news, it needed a new clutch. I really didn't want to spend any money on it, but I had no option, I needed it. Not only for my daily commute but also to visit Mum, and to be fair it was sometimes my escape.

I headed straight for the staff room when I eventually made it to work, grabbed a coffee and found a quiet corner to sit in. Everyone seemed a bit cliquey here, they all got together and chatted about their weekend or work, and I didn't seem to fit in anywhere. No one seemed to be paying me much attention, not that I wanted any really, I guess I just wanted to fit in. I suppose they would get used to me one day and I'd be invited to join one of their groups.

Fortunately, one of my favourite past times is to people watch. I like to try and suss them out, imagine what sort of a person they are, who they live with and what sort of life they have.

Mr Bennett was Head of Science and seemed like a quiet man, probably in his late fifties. He had a good head of hair, grey with a dash of his natural colour black going through it, giving him a bit of a mad professor look about him. He obviously lived on his own and had most likely never had children. I felt there might be a different side to him, but I wasn't sure what. He seemed like someone who stayed in every night watching television, not that there is anything wrong with that, but I guessed he was a bit of a loner.

Then there was Miss Walker, she took drama which was very much reflected in her style. I think she lived a colourful life, was about forty-ish and from the things she said I think she had a girlfriend. She was very hippy looking, a free spirit, a bit like my Aunty Lesley used to be.

"Morning Lizzie"

I jumped as I felt a hand placed on my shoulder, it was Sebastian (or Seb as he was best known). He was Head of the Art department, and although he wasn't drop dead gorgeous, there was something about him. He was nearly six feet tall and had a cheeky look, with a likeness of Jack Sparrow about him. I could just imagine him with his famous hat in place and a cutlass in his hand, I chuckled inside as I thought about it. Suddenly I was snapped out of my wandering thoughts.

"So, how's it going?" Seb asked.

"Oh, sorry I was miles away"

"I can see that! I was just wondering if you are settling in? Do you feel like you're getting to know everyone now?"

I smiled up at him. "Yes, I think so… well a little anyway. I just need to get used to everything and everyone, but I'm sure I will be fine here."

"Yeah, it's difficult starting in a new school, I should know I've worked in a few. Maybe we should organise a night out with everyone, so you can get to know us all a bit better, I'll sort it" He smiled back and gently squeezed my shoulder before leaving the staff room to head for his first lesson.

I could see Mr Bennet making a beeline for me, so I quickly jumped up and went to wash my cup in the sink before heading to my own classroom.

This new school was an old-style school, probably built some time before the fifties. Some effort had been made to modify and modernise it, but thankfully it still held its character. My classroom was quite spacious, with large old-fashioned windows along one wall, making it freezing cold in winter and boiling hot in summer.

Today was a hot day, too hot to be stuck indoors. I was taking a class of around twenty students, we were studying psychology. I had given everyone an assignment to write, an analysis on 'The theories of Freud' Looking around the room I could see that most of the students were head down and concentrating, while others were clearly not, playing on their mobile phones and no doubt catching up with social media.

As my eyes glanced back towards what I was doing they paused over Will, his head was down, and he was busy writing away, he didn't notice me taking him in. He was so fit and was full of testosterone, he caught my eye the moment I came to St Martin's. His chestnut brown hair complimented his bronze complexion, his muscular taught torso pressed up against his crisp white shirt, I could see the beads of sweat glistening on his chest.

I got out my seat and made my way to the back of the classroom, checking on the progress of the students' work. As I walked past Will his scent aroused me, I breathed it in and briefly closed my eyes as I made my way back to my desk. I picked up my pencil and fondled it as my mind wandered. I imagined that I was in the local park when I unexpectedly bumped into Will.

"Hi Miss Vaughn"

"Please, call me Lizzie" I smiled.

We strolled around the park and chatted, it was a swelteringly hot day but unusually the park was deserted. Eventually we came to a standstill near an old tree, Will leaned forward and gave me a lingering kiss. I pulled away from him abruptly, knowing that we surely couldn't do this, but my senses were aroused so I pulled him back towards me and closer than before. He moved his hand slowly onto my thigh, desperately grasping at the hem of my skirt, seeking for the naked flesh underneath His large hand caressed the top of my thigh, I gasped with excitement and anticipation.

He slowly eased his hand between my legs, slipped his finger into my damp panties and inserted it into me. I squirmed, feeling him move inside me, crying out at each thrust. I could feel his cock as he pressed himself up against me, hard and erect, waiting to be released like a caged animal. I let out a scream as I reached my climax.

Will moved around me so that he was resting his back against the tree, I flicked open the metal button on his jeans and released him. Dropping to my knees in front of him, I place my lips on him firmly, taking him all…

Back in the classroom as I am thinking of this I curl my lips around the pencil I am holding, gripping it firmly between my teeth I hold it tighter, and as I do it snaps in my hand, bringing me crashing back down to earth. I look around the room to see if anyone noticed and seem to have caught the attention of a couple of students, who find it rather amusing. Red-faced I nod for them to get on with their work. I glance across at Will and decide it would be better to leave my fantasies about him at home.

I guess he reminded me a lot of Paul, he had the same physique and he had his good looks too. I thought back to when Paul and I met for the first time. It was in a local pub, just a random night out with a few friends. He was a friend of one of the guys we hung around with, he had been away for a couple of years working abroad and was a personal trainer to someone in Australia. Why he came back I'll never know, but apparently, he had always said it was only ever going to be a temporary thing.

We hit it off straight away. He was tall, muscular, tanned and blonde - what's not to like? He had the most beautiful ice blue eyes which I loved at first, but grew to hate, as they could turn a woman's head the minute he looked at them.

After that night we became inseparable, we found a flat and moved in together within months. Mum wasn't too happy, she wanted me to do it all the right way, engagement, marriage etc. He did buy me a ring but that was it really, nothing fancy. But then I didn't want anything else, I just wanted him. A couple of years later he came home from work one day and asked if I fancied going to Gretna Green for a few days.

I laughed and asked, "Why are we getting married?"

He looked across at me and smiled, "Is that a yes before I even ask then?"

I threw my arms around him and he swung me around, I couldn't believe it, how romantic! I never imagined that he would ever ask me to marry him, I thought we would always just live together.

Paul had managed to get a post at Greenhill Comprehensive, the same school as me, doing physical education. Because of this it meant we had to wait until the school holidays before we could go to Gretna.

I remember our wedding like it was yesterday, we bought cheap rings from the jewellers on the high street and set off for Gretna. I wore a cream, polka dot knee-high dress and Paul just wore trousers, shirt and a tie. I said that he should wear a kilt, I still remember the look he gave me before I laughed back at him. We had a couple of strangers as witnesses, and even though it was very quick it was perfect for us. Afterwards, we went for a meal and downed a bottle of cheap champagne in our room. It was our perfect day, it was our perfect wedding.

The place we stayed was lovely, an old-style bed and breakfast, it was a bit like stepping back in time. Heavy lined green curtains hung from the rails, there was a large four poster bed and an enormous roll top bath. We stayed a couple of days and spent most of it in the room.

Paul always seemed to do the right thing, he knew just how to please me. One night while we were there he ran a bath for me, filled it almost to the brim with steaming hot water and a gorgeous smelling bubble bath, there were bubbles everywhere. He had placed candles all around the room, it was so romantic. As we both climbed in it the water nearly ran over the edge and making love in a bath is never easy. It wasn't long before the water began to spill over the sides, splashing onto the floor, putting out most of the candles as it did so. We soon abandoned the whole idea and made our way to the bedroom.

Still soapy we slipped on the wooden floor and came crashing down. We lay out on the cold floorboards laughing, Paul cupped my face with his hand and kissed me. His warm lips gently brushed against my skin,

I ran my hands over the curves of his strong wet muscular back, and as his torso pressed against me my breasts ached to be touched. The touch of his lips on my neck left me aroused, wanting him inside me, I could feel he felt the same.

We spun around and suddenly I was on top, slowly easing myself onto him, sliding back and forth. I filled with excitement. Gently rocking, I could feel every sense inside me peaking and slowly getting ready to burst. The culmination of everything I'd felt that day welled up inside me and then just like that I came, my orgasm letting Paul know exactly how I was feeling.

I rolled off to the side and once again lay on the cold wooden floor. Paul held his hand out towards me, I caught hold of it and he led me over to the four-poster bed. As I lay myself in position in the centre of it, Paul grabbed one of my body lotions and squirted it over me. I squealed and laughed playfully as the cold lotion hit my skin. Sitting astride me he began to gently smooth the lotion all over my body. Closing my eyes, I could feel his strong hands feeling their way around, it felt so good. His hard cock was pressing up against me once again, he was eager and ready to go.

His torso slid up and down my body, slowly teasing me with his motion, I caught hold of his hand and guided it towards my aching wet pussy. His finger slid along my clitoris, he gently rubbed it and I could feel it tingling. I was just about to climax when he entered me. With an unbelievably powerful rhythm, Paul made love to me, his deep thrusts made my toes curl and I could feel that familiar rush once more. My body became rigid as I felt that surge of pleasure fill me.

We were good together, I felt we had everything and more. I loved him more than anything and anyone else. We were with each other for about eight years, and it was perfect – at least it was until she came along.

Chapter Three

On Monday morning I arrived at work a little earlier than usual so decided to spend some time relaxing and planning my day of teaching in the staff room. I was just making myself a second cup of tea when Seb came over to me.

"Lizzie, how about Saturday?"

"Sorry?" I asked, slightly confused.

"Saturday for a night out? You know, a work do… the chance to get to know us all?"

"Erm yes, I think I can do Saturday" I lied, looking upwards as if I was thinking hard about what I had planned. I knew that I could meet him really, I didn't have much going on in my social life anymore, it was pretty rubbish.

"Great, we'll sort out the finer details on Friday" he smiled at me.

"Yes, that's fine, I look forward to it" I smiled back.

Friday came and as promised we sat together briefly at lunch and arranged to meet on the Saturday at the Red Lion pub in town. Seb gave me his number in case there were any changes to the plan. I wasn't sure that I wanted to go now, it had seemed like a good idea at the time, but the thought of having to spend the night making small talk with everyone filled me with dread. Mr Bennett, Miss Walker and a couple of other teachers were going to be there, none of which I had not even spoken to really, nothing more than a hello anyway.

When Saturday came I was tempted to ring Seb and say I couldn't make it, but Caroline had what she called 'a word with me' and told me it was just what I needed. So, there I was making my way into the town on the same bus I had been catching every morning for work. The journey was very different on an evening, or should I say the people were. Everyone was all dressed up, busily chatting about their forthcoming evening, a buzz flowing through the air that you couldn't help but feel too. There was an interesting mixture of scents - light, floral perfumes and strong, heady colognes. I smiled to myself, it was a long time since I had been out, and I realised I was missing it.

I arrived at the Red Lion for seven thirty, it was a lot busier than I thought it would be. I couldn't see anyone I recognised from work sat at any of the tables, so I made my way straight over to the bar instead. I ordered half a lager, not my usual tipple but I knew wine would go straight to my head, and I didn't want to show myself up with people I barely knew.

I felt some hands grab my waist.

"Hey, how are you doing?" It was Seb, his dark hair naturally fell onto his forehead in small curls, his eyes were brown like the richest chocolate, he was wearing blue worn jeans and a white linen shirt.

"I'm fine - would you like a drink?" I asked.

"No, I'll get these"

"I've already ordered, what would you like?" I insisted.

"Ok, white wine please" Seb grinned, and I couldn't help but wonder why I had never fully noticed how attractive he was before.

I grabbed the drinks and Seb led the way to where the others were sat.

"Ok, so let's introduce you properly to everyone - this is Julie or Mrs Lancaster"

We both exchanged a hi to each other.

"And this is John, aka Mr Parsons" John held his hand out, "Nice to meet you"

"And you already know Bernadette and Geoff" I smiled across at them.

Everyone began chatting with each other, I tried to include myself in the conversation, but it just wasn't happening and after a while I began to feel a bit left out. Seb tried to include me a couple of times but I just wasn't feeling it. I looked down at my glass, it was empty.

"Anyone ready for a drink?"

They almost all replied in unison, claiming they would get their own. I made my way over to the bar, 'they didn't even want me to buy them a drink'. I thought about slipping away and I was just about to do so when I heard "Are you ok?"

It was Julie.

"Yeah I'm fine thank you"

"You'll soon get used to us all you know, it's awful when you start a new place, and everyone's a bit cliquey here"

She could say that again. I think she was a similar age to me, Julie, possibly a bit older in her mid-thirties. While we waited to be served she filled me in on the gossip and gave me the low down on the staff, in particular on Bernadette and Seb. I was right about Bernadette she did have a girlfriend, she was forty-six and apparently wanted to ditch her job and take off in her campervan with her. Seb was surprisingly single, he was the free spirit in the staff room. Julie had a bloke but nothing serious, she was a bit like me only she had lived with someone for a few years, but it didn't work out. He had been married before and went back to his wife after getting his fill from her.

I confessed to her that I was thinking of going home.

"Don't go home, just give it a bit longer! Do you like jaeger?"

"Jaeger bombs? Not done them for a while, but yeah, why not!"

She ordered them, and we quickly knocked them back, I was beginning to feel better already. We made our way back to the rest of them, Seb caught sight of us first.

"Here they are! Where have you two been? We thought you had gone home!"

Julie and I glanced at each other and began to laugh. "No, I was just filling Lizzie in on the gossip on everyone"

"And you're still here!" Everyone laughed.

Julie and I got into rounds with the odd shot thrown in and the evening became more relaxed as it went on. We moved from bar to bar, Julie and I holding each other up. We finally ended up in the Wine Cellar, which was quite a new bar, one that I had never been in. It was just after midnight and Julie got up to declare she was leaving.

"Look I'm gonna get off, I've had enough"

"Aww don't go yet!"

"No Lizzie I have to, have a good night and don't do anything I wouldn't do" She winked, gave me a hug along with everyone else and left.

Not long after John and Bernie also decided to go home leaving me, Seb and Geoff to go it alone.

"Do you fancy a nightcap?' Seb asked.

"Why not!?" I found myself saying, although I felt I had probably had enough already.

"We're gonna head off Geoff"

"Are we not gonna have one in here?" I asked.

"No, I have a nice bottle of wine we can polish off at home, I'm only up the road"

I grabbed my coat and picked my bag up. I looked over to Geoff who was staring deep into his pint glass, I wondered what he was thinking about. "See you on Monday then Geoff, nice to have met you properly"

"Yes Lizzie, nice night we must do another one soon, see you both Monday"

Mr Bennett - or should I say Geoff - was a lot nicer for knowing, and not the dark person I had imagined him to be. In fact, I can honestly say that I had really enjoyed my evening and was glad I had made the effort to go.

"Back to mine then?"

"Yes, why not!" I smiled.

"Let's crack that bottle of wine open"

No Rules

I never saw Seb as a wine drinker and was surprised that he was drinking it that night, he just didn't seem the type. I really wasn't sure I could manage any more alcohol, but I suppose I could try a glass.

Seb suggested we walk back to his place as it wasn't far. I think he lied, after what seemed like an age we finally arrived at his 'house', which as it turned out was more of an attic bedsit. We entered the main door and ahead of me was a badly lit flight of stairs. I gingerly followed him up and when we reached the top we made our way down a corridor to be met by a second flight of stairs.

"God, you must be fit living here" I half panted. I could hear Seb laughing, I could hardly breathe.

As we reached the top I heard him say, "Just one more flight"

"You're kidding! Where do you live? In the attic?"

"Yeah…" he looked sheepish and scratched at the back of his head.

"Well I hope you've got some oxygen on tap when we get there!"

As we turned the corner there was another staircase, this one narrower than the others. I cautiously followed him up the wooden steps, and we continued until we reached what I can only describe as a cupboard door. But when Seb opened it up it was like Narnia, albeit a very messy Narnia.

"Come in" he said, his hand sweeping across to welcome me in.

There was a small dormer window to the right of the room. I went over, stood on my tiptoes and peered out of it to check out the view. It looked out onto the main road, it was quiet out there, with no cars going by apart from the odd taxi.

A wooden floor lay under my feet, with a large fluffy circular rug in the middle of the room, covered in bits of fluff and looking like a rather neglected dog. There was a small two-seater sofa randomly placed next to it, which looked like it had originated from the seventies, and a couple of worn leather looking bean bags. I thought about sitting on one of the bean bags, but I wasn't sure that I would be able to get back up again. I took my jacket off and sat on the edge of the sofa instead, clumsily discarded my heels and relaxed back into the cushions. I was happy to be relieved of my shoes, though very nice they had proven to be quite impractical for the amount of walking and dancing we had been doing around town.

Seb slipped his own jacket off, threw it onto the nearest chair and headed over to the fridge to grab the wine. The tiny kitchen was incorporated into the main room of the bedsit and it didn't take long to search the cupboards for a couple of glasses. They were probably mostly in the sink, judging by the pile of pots I could see. He eventually came towards me with a couple of half pints of wine, I could already feel the effects of the hangover I would reap tomorrow.

Seb sat on the floor resting his back on the sofa, he handed me my half-pint of wine and I took a sip.

"So how are you feeling now?"

"Pretty good actually"

He laughed, "No, I mean now you've got to know everyone"

"Oh, right sorry" I smiled back at him as if I was teasing, my head was spinning like a fairground ride out of control. I forced myself to focus on what Seb had asked me. "Yeah I've enjoyed it, everyone is quite nice"

"Quite nice!" he laughed.

"Well you know what I mean! I wasn't expecting to get on with everyone, they all seemed a bit cliquey" I pulled a face.

"Well you seemed to get on quite well with Julie"

"Aww I like Julie, she's great" I took another large gulp of wine.

"Yeah, she is. They just need to get to know you a bit better, that's all"

"Yes, I guess so… Mr Bennetts not how I expected him to be"

"Old Geoff… yes he's a dark horse, but he's a genuine sort of guy"

"What do you mean dark horse?" I asked.

"Well he quite likes a party. He doesn't get out much, so when he does he lets his hair down a bit"

So, I was right with my theory he stays in quite a lot, a bit of a loner. "So, he prefers his own company?"

"No quite the opposite but he doesn't get much chance as he looks after his wife, she's disabled. I'm not sure what her disability is but I know he's always busy with her"

"No children then?"

"Yeah two, both at uni, he was adamant that their mum's illness wouldn't infringe on their prospects"

I suddenly felt hot like I was going to pass out, either that or I was going to throw up. "Can I use your loo please?"

"Sure, just through that door"

Another door that looked like a cupboard but hid what was quite a big bathroom. A frosted window on one wall, with no curtains, and just a toilet, sink and shower. I fumbled for the zip on my jeans and quickly pulled them down. I sunk down heavily onto the toilet seat, hitting the back of the cistern with force. Holding my head in my hands I desperately tried to focus my eyes. I really shouldn't drink wine, in the words of UB40, it goes to my head.

I reached for the loo roll and then flushed, pushing myself back up off the loo. I stood at the sink and washed my hands, glancing up at the mirror, I rubbed my wet hands over my face. I needed to sober up.

When I got back into the room, Seb was looking through a plastic box on the floor.

"Have you lost something?" I asked.

"A record" he replied.

"I love that record player"

"Good isn't it, I picked it up in Camden market a while back, it's a genuine one and in mint condition. Ah here it is!"

As I sank back onto the couch he held up an album that was familiar to me from when I was a child, and although my head was a little fuzzy it brought back lots of memories. "The best of bread, I remember my mum playing that all the time when I was young"

He looked across and smiled. "Me too" He carefully placed the needle onto the record and came back to sit on the floor. I shuffled off the couch to join him.

"Do you know Lizzie I love this album, reminds me of when I was a kid"

"Yeah I know what you mean"

We sat and chatted about when we were young and the different things we had got up to. I discovered that Seb was four years younger than me, and as Julie had said, he was a free spirit. I glanced down at my watch and noticed it was nearly one am.

"I best be heading off soon" I said, stifling a yawn.

"One for the road?"

I looked at my watch again as if to clarify that it was late. As I lifted my head back up I noticed him looking at me, his eyes smouldering, and the devilish side of my conscience pointed out to me that I didn't need to be up in the morning.

I handed my glass to Seb. "Just a small one"

He came back with what he perceived to be a small one and sat down beside me, handing me the glass.

I rested my head against his shoulder, "I've enjoyed tonight, thank you, it's just what I needed"

"Me too, and it's not over yet…"

Chapter Four

Seb slipped his arm around my shoulder and kissed my head. I looked up at him, the atmosphere in the room had changed dramatically and I could sense where the night would be taking us. I wondered if he could tell just by the look in my eye that I wanted this just as bad as he seemed to.

He kissed me gently on the lips, and as I kissed him back he slid his hand around my waist. He pulled away and slowly traced his lips over my neck, sending a sensation through me that I hadn't felt, in what felt like a long time. He reached for the hem of my t-shirt and pulled it up with a hint of urgency, tugging it over my breasts and revealing most of my chest, searching to caress my breast over my bra.

Kissing my cleavage whilst pulling the shirt further up and over my head, Seb released the clasp to my bra and removed it with ease. His hand tightened around my waist and he moaned into my ear. An overwhelmingly strong wave of desire coursed through my body. His hot hand slowly glided over my bare skin, gently touching the curves of my breast. We were soon laid on the floor, grinding against one another, feeling the full force of each other's body. The scent of his musk aftershave was enticing. I wanted to feel every bit of him, naked, closer to me, inside me.

We moved around whilst he fumbled to undo the fastening on my jeans, eventually flicking the button open and pulling the zipper down, he began to slide his hand into the waistband.

Suddenly he stopped. "Wait" He scrambled to his feet and held his hand out to me. "Come on"

I grabbed his hand and he pulled me up to standing, leading me into his bedroom. As he opened the door I noticed the room was already lit by a small lamp on his bedside table. It appeared to be a naked woman holding a bulb, and looked handmade, possibly one of his projects in school. The room smelt a bit stale, the true whiff of a single man, but the scent of his musk aftershave overpowered it just enough to mask it slightly.

There was an old wooden bed against the facing wall, unmade, covered with a black sheet and matching quilt cover, typical bloke bedding. Seb positioned himself on the bed like some sort of chauvinistic Greek god, I should have known at that moment that it was time to go home. I could have listened to my conscience, but did I? Did I hell.

"Come here" He beckoned me across to him.

My head was still fuzzy with a mixture of beer, Jaeger and cheap wine, and way too muddled to be having sex with the guy I worked alongside at school. Despite this I crawled onto the bed, on my hands and knees towards him, in the distance David Gates was still playing.

A stray lock of Seb's chestnut brown hair gently fell onto his forehead, his smile captured me again, I ran my fingers through his hair as I pulled his head towards me. We began to kiss again, his hands gently eased my jeans down, leaving my thong in full view. Not my best one I agree, but clearly, I was not expecting this. He tugged at it and pulled it down over my feet, his lips gently brushed against my body as he moved back up, and our lips met again. I ran my tongue over his smooth almost perfect teeth, I really wanted him now, little did I know what was about to happen.

His fingers slowly made their way over my aching body, slipping between my thighs and entering deep inside me with ease. There was no need for any further foreplay, I was ready now. He pushed my legs open, his head of curly hair brushed against the top of my thighs as he kissed my legs. His tongue found me, teased me and made me need him more.

I reached down cupping his head in my hands, "Come here".

He smiled back at me, "Not yet, we've got plenty of time, in fact, all night"

I slipped my hand between his legs and wrapped my hand around his clean-shaven balls. I moved my hand and ran it along his shaft, holding him tight between my finger and thumb. I moved my head between his legs and now my hair was brushing against his inner thighs. As I ran my lips over him he shuddered with excitement. He spun around and suddenly we were both enjoying the fullness of each other.

I began to push down on him faster, and as in response he licked me harder, drinking me in. I could feel my orgasm building up inside me, until once again he stopped. Following his lead, I stopped too, looking over at him to see where this was heading to next. He flipped me over onto my back. For a moment I lay breathless, wondering where this was going, and then with the palm of his hands he opened my legs, exposing me to the cold air of his room. The change in temperature added to the intense pleasure I was feeling.

I lay there like an outstretched Water Lily, waiting and wanting. His tongue explored the folds of the lily, this time with more precision and my heart was pounding now, pumping hard. This time there was no holding back, I was coming. I quivered as it revved up within, my toes curling, every muscle in my body pulsing and striving for pole position. He hit just the right spot and I screamed, letting go of all my tension. I yearned for more. I lay back in the comfort of my serenity and could have easily drifted off to sleep.

Seb smiled at me, "You ok?"

I smiled and nodded back to him, he kissed me softly, his lips were like crushed velvet as they touched mine. His hands once again working their way back down between my legs, he opened them up and slowly moved them above my head. His hand gently slid down my right leg till it reached my already wet clitoris, as he searched for the spot he began rubbing back and forth with a gentle motion. I wasn't sure I could take it just yet, but as he continued I felt myself building back up to another orgasm. His fingers entered me, and I let out a brief moan as he does so.

"Oh, oh-oh God no, please"

"Hmm, you like that yeah?"

"Yes, oh yes"

"Come on, can you feel it coming?"

"Yes, yes I can but I want to wait" I say panting in between.

"Don't hold it, don't wait, let it go" He whispers to me.

As I let out a cry he enters me, pushing hard. I can feel him hard inside me, moving back and forth, faster and faster. Eventually we reach a climax together, something I had genuinely never done before.

We both relax back onto the bed, our bodies dripping with sweat.

Within five minutes he was ready again, that night, and through till the early hours of the morning we managed positions I had never dreamed of. I felt like we had put the karma sutra to shame. Around 4am we finally lay together exhausted and I drifted off to sleep.

I woke up during the night and fumbled around in the dark looking for the door to the lounge, I needed the toilet. The more I tried not to make a noise the more I made, Seb moaned a little and I thought I'd woken him, but he rolled over and continued snoring.

It was cold now in the flat, the heat from our evening of passion had melted away and the heating was off for the night. Plus, I assumed all the alcohol I had consumed had worn off. I hurried back into the bedroom and as I lay back in bed I noticed a skylight above me. The sky was clear, and the stars were flickering. I could understand why he liked living here, even if it was only for this view.

When I woke in the morning I was alone in bed, but I could hear Seb in the room next door. I searched for my clothes but could only find my thong and jeans. Remembering that my bra and t-shirt were in the next room, I picked up one of Seb's shirts from the floor and put it on. I awkwardly walked through to the living room, Seb was laid on the couch reading a newspaper and the radio played in the distance.

"Hi, Coffee?" he asked nonchalantly.

"No, I'll have a tea please" I replied. I felt quite awkward and embarrassed, whilst Seb didn't seem at all phased by anything. He got up and made his way to the kitchen area and flicked the kettle on. I noticed my bra and t-shirt still lay on the floor, I quickly picked them up and rolled my bra up into my t-shirt.

"Sit down" he gestured towards the sofa "did you sleep ok?"

"Yes, thanks, when I eventually got to sleep"

He grinned and winked before returning to the kettle. "Sugar?"

"No thanks"

"So, what you up to today?" he asked.

"Well, I was going to pop and see my Mum, but I don't think I'll get there now"

"Where does your Mum live?"

"Nottingham"

"Oh, right, so not around the corner"

"No, well it's about 30 miles away. I don't get there as often as I would like, what are your plans today?"

"Nothing, absolutely nothing, I might nip for one in the local this evening, or I might just stay in and get my marking done"

We made small talk for the next half hour before I went to the loo and finished getting dressed. My head was pounding, and I looked a mess, totally dishevelled. I needed to get home. I hung Seb's shirt over the towel rail in the bathroom and did my best to make myself look decent enough to leave.

When I came back into the living room Seb was laid out again with his paper. I looked for my shoes and reached for my jacket that had fallen behind the couch.

"Right I better be off, thanks for the tea" I smiled at Seb.

"Ok" He threw his paper down and jumped off the sofa to see me out. "See you Monday then" He held the door open, I walked towards him and leaned forward with the intention of giving him a kiss on the cheek, which sadly turned out to be an awkward hug.

I felt myself flush with embarrassment. "Yes, see you Monday" I managed to say avoiding eye contact.

I began to make my way down the wooden stairs and heard him close the door behind me. I finally came to the end of the dodgy staircase and reached the main door onto the street. I realised I was a bit far away from home so decided to call a taxi.

I arrived back home in no time, there was no sign of Caroline, so I assumed she must have stayed over at Jim's again. I searched the fridge for something to eat but there was nothing, neither of us bothered to do much food shopping.

I fancied something stodgy, something that would soak up all the alcohol that was tormenting my body and causing me to have this horrendous hangover. Then I remembered I was sure I had seen some sausages in the freezer, that should do it. I rummaged around in the freezer drawers until I found them in the last one, right at the back. I popped them into the microwave to defrost, then stuck them under the grill.

I eventually settled down with my sandwich, a nice cup of tea and a rom-com. I couldn't concentrate on the film all that much, my mind kept drifting back to the previous night. I became engulfed with embarrassment, I hardly knew Seb really and I had just spent the night with him, and on top of that, I had to see him at work again on Monday. If I was honest though I did enjoy his company, and the whole evening was just what I needed.

For the rest of the weekend I decided to stay in and catch up with my marking, so I grabbed my self a glass of white wine and concentrated on the chore in hand.

Monday came all too soon and before I knew it I was heading out to the car. I was feeling quite nervous at the thought of seeing Seb again, but I needn't have. I walked into the staff room, he was already there chatting to Geoff and didn't seem to even notice me enter the room. With my head down, I dashed over to where the kettle was and flicked the switch on. I searched for my mug in the cupboard but as usual it wasn't there. I quickly scanned the room but couldn't see anyone clutching it. I grabbed the first one I could see instead and gave it a quick swill out.

The place was untidy, an opened jar of coffee was on the side and tea bags were just scattered all over the work surface instead of tucked away neatly in their box. I reached for one of them and dropped it in my cup.

With my hands pressed against the work surface I leaned closer to the window, looking out onto the school yard. I tried to look like I was completely cool with the situation. I was in fact wondering if Seb would even look at me, never mind acknowledge me, or whether he would act like nothing had happened.

An unexpected voice came from behind and startled me. "Morning!"

It was Julie, she grabbed a mug out of the cupboard, tipped a generously heaped spoon of coffee out of the already opened jar and leaned against the work surface next to me.

"So how was it then?"

I looked back at her. "How was what?"

"Friday, you and Seb, did you go back to his?" she grinned.

I could feel myself blushing, the kettle clicked to signal it had boiled – perfect timing. I picked it up and filled my mug, my tea bag floated in the harsh limed water and I searched for a spoon. Anything to avoid making eye contact with her. If she could see my face I knew it would give everything away instantly.

"Milk?" Julie enquired, as she held the large carton over my tea.

"Yes please" I found a spoon and swirled it round my mug.

"I take it you would rather not say"

"No, it's not that, I don't mind but just not here"

"That's fine do you fancy a drink after work? Give me all the gory details"

I looked back onto the school yard wondering if Seb had even noticed I had walked in.

"Well? Are we on then?"

"Yes, yes that's fine"

"Ok we'll make final arrangements later. Oh, look out, the studs on his way see you! Bye!"

I hardly got chance to reply before I felt Seb sidle up to me. "Hi, you ok?"

He dropped his mug into the sink and I could feel a rush of colour flush back into my cheeks. "Yes, thank you I'm fine, and you?"

"All good thanks, had a heavy weekend mind but I survived" he smiled, a knowing glimmer flashed in his eyes.

"Oh good, sorry but I best go, I've got a few things to prep for my lesson" I quickly swilled my mug with hot water, stood it on the drainer and left the room.

As I wandered back to my classroom I couldn't help feeling that everyone had been staring at me in the staff room, and that they were all aware of what had happened between me and Seb. Of course, my mind was working overtime as usual and I was imagining all sorts of rumours. Mind you to be fair, they wouldn't have really been rumours.

The day seemed to drag on for what felt like an eternity, I just wanted to get my lessons over with and leave the day behind me. I went out at lunch time as I didn't feel like facing everyone in the staff room again. I had a packed lunch with me, so I walked over to the local park, mulling everything over in my mind along the way.

I don't know why I felt so hung up about it, I guess it's because it wasn't my usual style. I didn't normally hook up with someone then shag them on the first date, and come to think of it, we hadn't even had a date.

Chapter Five

That evening I met Julie at the same bar we had all previously met in on our night out, she was there when I got there, half a lager in hand.

"Hi! Excuse the state of me, I didn't go home after school finished. I thought I'd stay and prep for tomorrow, will save me coming in so early"

I smiled at her, "I'll just get a drink"

I made my way over to the bar, wondering what I should tell Julie. Do I tell her the truth? That we made out all night? Or do I lie and say nothing happened? No, she would see right through me, she knows him too well. Plus, I can tell that she knows exactly what happened, she just wants the juicy details. I grabbed my drink and wandered back to where Julie was sitting.

"So, come on, spill the beans, did you end up back at his?" she asked, before I'd even had chance to sit down and make myself comfy.

I took a sip of my drink and looked up at her. "Might have" I replied, with a little smile, feeling sheepish.

"Oh, come on! Didn't he take you up to his love nest? Or should I say attic..." Julie started to laugh.

I laughed with her, but I began to feel embarrassed, I was beginning to think that Julie had been there before me. As the conversation unfurled it became apparent that I was right, Julie had been there before me. Her and Seb had had a one-night stand a while back, a bit like mine.

"Sorry I should have told you that night - warned you in fact - it's just I didn't want to interfere. I mean I could see you were into him and who am I to spoil someone else's fun?"

I looked up at her. "So, who's fun would that be, his or mine?"

She laughed. "Well both of you I guess, you're both old enough to know what you were – or should I say WHO you were doing"

She was right we were both old enough, and it was my own doing, well mine and the demon drink.

I woke up the next day with a sense of dread filling my stomach, I really didn't want to go to work. I felt like things would be awkward with Julie now, as well as Seb. But I made the journey in and it wasn't as bad as I was expecting, Julie beckoned me straight over to sit with her in the staff room. I made myself a coffee then went over to settle myself into the seat. Then Seb came in.

"Alright girls" He nodded and smiled as he said it, I could have slapped him, he was so cocky. I wished I had never gone with him, but I couldn't undo what had been done, I just had to get on with my job.

Earlier in the week I had decided that I needed to have a night out and truly let my hair down. Fortunately, my friend Chrissie was available and was on the same wavelength, so we arranged to go out on the Friday night.

Chrissie was a great friend, always there for me when I needed someone. She had a husband and two lovely children, but she was always there for me no matter what, and always had been.

We decided to go into the old part of town, mainly because I knew the pubs would be quieter, so I'd be able to pour my heart out to her and feel sorry for myself. Unfortunately, that night she was having none of it. Apparently, she had decided that I needed to forget about everything, have some fun and move on. We didn't end up talking much about anything apart from what shot to have next.

It was that night that I met Sam. We were in a small quaint pub, I was feeling sorry for myself and Chrissie kept changing the subject. I excused myself once I realised I wasn't going to get a proper chance to truly let all my feelings out and made my way up to the toilets. With it being a hundred or so years old pub, the toilets were quite out the way of the main bar area. Up a couple of flights of stairs, and down a small dingy passage which eventually led to the toilets. The gents were on the left and all in darkness, and the ladies a little further down on the right.

As I left the loo, I walked passed the gents still in darkness when a guy said.

"I can't find a light anywhere"

I was so startled I let out a scream, and then began to laugh.

"I'm so sorry I didn't mean to scare you, I just can't find a switch anywhere" he said in a deep, sexy voice.

"It's ok" I said still clutching my chest.

I returned to my seat and started telling my friend what had happened. We were both laughing about it when the same guy walked past. He sat down in a seat across from us, I hadn't noticed him there before. He looked over at me smiling and shaking his head and mouthed "I am so sorry".

I smiled back at him and replied, "it's fine really".

He was unshaven with the deepest brown eyes, he smiled again at me and I thought how dark and mysterious he seemed. But not in a bad 'I'm going to murder you' kind of way, in an 'I'm going to screw your brains out' exciting kind of way. I turned to Chrissie and she gave me a knowing smile.

"What?" I asked.

"Hmm get you, I think you're in there!"

"No way, he's just being nice because of what happened"

"Well, he's coming over"

I looked up just as he stopped in front of me. "Can I buy you girls, a drink?"

"No, it's fine, thank you" I replied.

"Aww come on! It's the least I can do" His deep brown eyes looked straight back at me, and well, I guess I melted. "Yes, ok thank you, just two halves of cider please"

As he left for the bar Chrissie said "You're a bit slow, you should have got a couple of shorts"

"No, I couldn't do that"

While he was at the bar I quickly finished off explaining what had happened, she was still laughing as he returned from the bar. "I'm guessing she's told you how we met, I'm Sam by the way" He smiled and extended his hand out to me.

"Lizzie" I said, taking in the weight and feel of his hand as he shook mine.

"Hi Lizzie"

Before I could introduce her Chrissie said, "I'm Chrissie, nice to meet you" She grabbed hold of his hand using a force like one of the vices Mr Jones uses in his woodwork department. "So, are you married then?"

He paused for a second and glanced at me to catch my reaction. "Do I honestly look married to you?"

"I don't know, what does married look like?" She laughed.

Sam was laughing too and pulling a face, my face flushed with embarrassment and I inwardly cringed as Chrissie's line of questioning continued.

"You haven't really answered my question…" she said with a cheeky smile on her face.

"No, I'm not married, never have been. Not met the right one yet I guess" he said glancing in my direction again, I felt myself go even redder and I felt butterflies fluttering away in my stomach.

Chrissie was oblivious and continued to talk his ear off all night, I'm surprised that I ever saw him again. But luckily for me I did, so there must have been something there. I started seeing Sam regularly after that night.

One night we arranged to go for one of our usual date nights. He was late picking me up and got to mine around 8:15pm, he didn't come in just blew his car horn and waited for me out front. I'd been sat ready and waiting since 7:30pm, passing the time by chatting to Caroline about life.

"Right, looks like he's here FINALLY. See you later Caroline"

"Yeah see you later, have a good night" she replied, smiling over at me from the sofa as I headed out into the hall towards the front door.

I made my way out to the car, noticing that Sam was quite spruced up this evening, wondering if I needed to go back in and change. "You look smart, going anywhere nice?"

"Don't I always look nice then?" he flashed a grin, his eyes twinkling underneath the light as I opened the car door.

"Well yes, but you look like you've made an extra effort tonight"

"I don't know how to take that"

I looked across and laughed at him "No, you know what I mean!"

"Well I thought we could have a quick drink somewhere then go to the casino for a change"

I had never been to the casino before, so I was keen to give it a try. We drove to our usual little pub in the country, it was a cold frosty evening, but The Dog and Duck had a roaring open fire which we secured a seat next to.

I had been seeing Sam for around five months now and I was beginning to feel settled. We got on well, I guess we felt comfortable together, we seemed to like the same things and Sam had the same zest for life as me.

We had a couple of drinks in the pub, well I did, Sam was driving, and he would never drink and drive. He couldn't risk his licence with his job. He was an area manager for a large retail company, decent wage I think, he never gave much away, played his cards close to his chest.

"So, do you go to the casino a lot?" I asked.

"Occasionally, when I'm feeling flush"

"Oh, so you're feeling flush, are you?"

"Let's say I got an extra bonus this month that's burning a hole in my pocket"

We eventually left The Dog and duck later that evening and drove to the casino, which was in the main town. It was a rather plush looking place with padded seating everywhere, I thought it felt a bit like a brothel in places. Not that I knew what one of those was like, the nearest I had ever seen to anything like that was when I went on a ferry trip to Amsterdam.

There were a few of us on a girly weekend so we just had a giggle really. I was amazed at all the women in windows, of all ages, shapes and sizes, it took me all my willpower not to just stand and stare at them. I just couldn't comprehend why anyone would do that, and why men would pay for sex, this led to a massive debate about the why's and wherefores of prostitutes with my friends. But at the end of the day, the whole weekend was an experience I will never forget.

We got a drink at the bar then went to choose a table to do a bit of gambling, there were around four different ones to choose from. I found a stool at one and suggested we sit there, Sam sat next to me and there was a spare seat to the left of me. He put fifty pounds in notes on the table and asked for a colour, I had no idea what he was talking about, but the croupier clearly did as he slid a large number of pink chips towards him.

"Which number would you like Lizzie?"

"Oh, any, you just choose one"

"No, it's your first time you might get lucky" he smiled at me.

"But I haven't got a clue!"

"Ok then, red or black?"

"Red"

Sam piled a stack of chips on red and we waited... "23 Red" the croupier announced. "Yes!!" Sam cheered,

"Have you won?" I asked.

"No, WE'VE won" he answered excitedly.

"It's probably just beginners' luck"

"Well, we'll soon see" With that, Sam piled everything he had won on black.

"Oh my god! I can't look, are you stupid?"

Sam just laughed, I glanced around the table and was amazed at the number of chips some people were betting. I couldn't even look at the table as the tiny silver coloured ball rolled around the wheel at an ever-decreasing speed. Everyone was so different, some not paying any attention to the table, while others were nervously waiting for that silver ball to come to a halt, passing their chips through their fingers back and forth. With that, Sam yelled 'yes' in my ear again. "You are joking! Have we won again?"

"Yes!" he shouted, fist pumping the air.

"How much?"

"Oh, I don't know, a good few pounds though! Let's do it again!" he was well and truly caught up in the game.

"Oh no, don't, you won't be that lucky!"

"I will, trust me"

I downed my drink to try and steady my nerves. "Can we get a drink first before you make any rash decisions?"

"No, we can't leave the table it will break the good luck"

I rolled my eyes and sunk back onto the stool near the table. I looked around and noticed a waitress hovering around with a silver tray. "Excuse me could I order some drinks please?"

"Certainly Madam, what would you like?" she replied politely. I ordered a couple of Bacardi and cokes, then Sam asked me.

"So, what number do you want? Or would you like to go red or black again?"

"I seriously don't mind, and I don't care really"

"Just choose for me please" he begged.

"Ok black"

"What! Again?"

"Yes, black"

"Ok. Black it is" Sam pushed his whole pile of chips onto the black diamond. I felt sick. God knows how much was on there.

Our drinks were served in no time, I took a sip out of mine and glanced around the table. As I did a guy sat down to the left of me, he smelt so good. I looked back towards the roulette table and the guy leant over to place his bets. As he slid his chips over onto the play area he came within an inch of my face. I breathed his scent in, glancing down at my glass, unable to look him in the face. Every time he moved his knee brushed against mine. Feeling a little flushed I looked down again at my glass hoping to hide my embarrassment.

A voice next to me asked "Would you mind?"

I looked up towards him, he was clean shaven and had black hair which was cropped quite short, giving me the impression that he was possibly in the forces. That could have just been my mind wandering, I could just imagine him in a uniform of some kind. "Sorry?"

"Don't be" He smiled as he replied. "Would you mind just putting this on twenty-six, I can't reach it"

"Oh, right, yes of course" The croupier called out last bets and I stood up and quickly placed his chip on number twenty-six.

I could feel his leg pressed up against mine and could feel myself becoming really turned on, this game was quite up close and personal. Once again, I glanced down, not daring to look while the ball was being placed into the wheel.

The croupier spun the wheel around and flicked the ball onto it, as it rolled around the wheel I could still smell the scent of the dark handsome stranger to the left of me. And then with a bang I came crashing back down to Earth as Sam said, "Oh yes!" once again.

I looked up and he had won again. "Right let's go get a drink" I said glancing up at Sam, who was smiling like a Cheshire cat, the one who had just got the cream. I looked back at the guy and he was smiling too, twenty-six had won. 'Thank you' he mouthed at me, I just smiled back at him.

We found a little corner in the bar area and settled down with a drink.

"What's wrong don't you like it here?"

"No, it's not that, it's just such a lot of money"

"It's fine, it's just a bit of fun. Besides, I can afford it."
"So, are you always this lucky?"
"No, I don't think I have ever won this much. I just had a feeling tonight, you were my lady luck"

I looked up and laughed at him.

"Aww come on! Don't spoil it!"

Chapter Six

We sat and enjoyed a few more glasses of Bacardi, and I was beginning to feel quite relaxed when Sam asked, "Do you fancy going to a hotel for the night?"

"A hotel! We could just go back to mine!"

"I know but Caroline is always there" he looked at me with a twinkle in his eyes.

"Not always, but yes she will be tonight. Couldn't we just go back to yours then?"

"We could but it's a bit far isn't it? Come on, where's your sense of adventure?"

"Yes true, ok we'll see"

Sam lived out of town, we never went to his to be fair, he always preferred to stay at mine as it was closer for him to get to work.

We left the casino and as we made our way back to the car we were approached by a guy handing out leaflets. "Two for the price of one tonight, just give the leaflet to the guy on the door"

Sam took the leaflet and began to read it as we continued to the car. "What's it for?" I asked.

"A lap dancing club, do you fancy it?"

I began to giggle "Me! What would I do in a lap dancing club?"

"Have a dance?"

I started to laugh.

"Women do go in you know"
"Really!"
"Yes, they do. Come on it's only up here, let's give it a go"

Before I knew it, we were at the door, Sam paid the money and we went in. The entrance was very dark, and we were led to the bar by a man in a suit. It all felt a bit more up-market than what I expected.

I ordered a medium sweet white wine while poor Sam was still on the soft drinks. There were around twenty-five or, so girls dressed in what I would call just their underwear and high stilettos. Sam nodded over to an empty corner for us to sit down in, my bottom only just touched the seat when we were approached by two girls, one at either side of us.

Nikita (I'm guessing that was her stage name) was chatting with me. "Have you been here before?"

"No, never" I wondered how come she didn't know, I thought she would have known the regulars and none regulars.

"No, me neither" she replied.

"Oh, so where do you normally work?" I asked.

"I usually do this, but I tour around a bit, so you meet new people all the time". She seemed like a nice person, I don't know what I was expecting. "So, do you want a dance?"

"Erm, no I don't think so" I blushed.

"I can do a double for you and your husband?"

"No thank you, and he's not my husband"

"Oh, I'm sorry I didn't mean to offend you, I just assumed, I'm sorry I shouldn't have"

"No, it's ok you didn't offend me" There was an awkward silence between us as we both looked around the room.

"I tell you what I'll leave you to soak up the atmosphere of the room and if you decide you would like a dance, just let me know"

"Ok thank you"

And with that, she was gone. I looked across at Sam and he was deep in conversation with one of the other girls, she leant forward and said something to him then left.

"So how did you get on?"

"Fine, she thought you were my husband"

Sam started to laugh. "And did you put her straight?"

"Yes, I did, she said she would do a double" I began to giggle again and took a large gulp of my wine.

"Well Katrina said she would do us a double too"

I nearly choked on my wine and began to laugh.

"If we go in you can't laugh"

"Who said I was going in?"

"You can't get this far and not give it a try"

"So, you come here regularly then?"

"No! Well I've never been to this one before"

"Oh, so you do go to lap dancing clubs?"

"I've been to a couple before but I'm not like a regular customer or anything" I glanced at Sam and I must have given him a knowing look. "Honestly, the first time was for a stag do and the second was with some workmates"

I looked up and laughed "It's fine I'm joking"

Just then another girl approached us. "Hi, my name is Lexie, what's your name?"

I didn't want to really give my name, I tried to think of one to say but I couldn't think of any and before I knew it I had blurted it out. "I'm Lizzie"

"Nice to meet you Lizzie, have you come for a lap dance this evening?"

I was just about to say no when Sam answered for me. "Yes, we have. Can we have a double, but I would just like to watch you on her"

"Certainly" she smiled "follow me"

I leant forward looking over at Sam, shooting him daggers with my eyes. He just smiled and winked back at me. I couldn't believe what he'd roped me into.

As she led us through a series of corridors to another room I nervously looked at Sam. "You'll be fine" he whispered.

Everything looked a bit seedy, well cloak and dagger I guess. We entered a small room leading off the one we had just entered. There was no door to it, just a metallic silver beaded curtain. I was surprised as it looked cheap in comparison to what I had already seen since we arrived.

Lexie said that we had to pay up front and my eyes widened as Sam handed over forty pounds. She had a small see-through clutch type bag that she slotted the money into. "Here let me take your bag" She lifted my bag from me and handed it over to Sam who was sat beside me. I must have looked like a rabbit caught in the headlights, I hadn't got a clue what was going to happen next, and I wasn't even sure why I was there.

"Could you rest your hands by your side please?"

I sniggered as I said "What? I'm not going to touch you!"

"It's just the club rules, we have to abide by them"

"Oh, I see" I flushed red with embarrassment. I did as she said. Some old school sexy R&B music began to play in the background, she turned her back to me and began to dance. She was wearing black hold up stockings with red seams up the back and high stiletto heels on with red soles, I was guessing that they were Louboutin's.

She was dark haired, quite petite and very young looking. A dark red lipstick coloured her full lips, her eyes were a deep rich brown, with perfect eyelashes that must have been false. She seductively moved her body from side to side, squirming around like a snake leaving its basket. She reached her hands around the back of her, she ran them over her tiny pert buttocks and glanced over her shoulder at me. I looked across to Sam and he nodded at me to watch her. She turned around to face me, still slithering around as she moved closer.

She looked straight at me as she began to undress, first slowly removing her bra. Leaning into me she brushed her lips against my earlobe, I closed my eyes and felt her hot breath against my skin, her sweet fragrance teased me. She pulled away and as I opened my eyes I caught her peeling off her pants, leaving her black seamed stockings in place.

I glanced over at Sam again in disbelief, I had always thought that they just danced at this sort of thing, I didn't know they stripped too, was I so naive? Sam smiled back at me and said. "Just enjoy it" I was feeling somewhat relaxed as the alcohol was beginning to take effect.

Lexie climbed up onto the chair that I was sat on, standing astride me, her smooth shaved pussy within an inch of my face. She rubbed herself in a circular motion almost right against me, leaving her scent in the air. As she slowly stepped down onto the floor her perfectly formed body brushed against me once more. Her hands explored her own body and she looked at me and licked her lips. Once again, she turned her back on me, bending forward, her hands sliding between her legs to tease me again, gently moving her fingers against her smooth silk pussy.

She stood herself upright and slapped her naked bottom unexpectedly and hard, I jumped and felt a giggle coming on. I glanced across at Sam who shook his head sternly at me and I just about managed to contain it. Lexie walked towards me and pushed herself against me, rubbing her breasts close to my face, her nipples slowly brushing against my cheek. My heart was racing, and I felt a tingling between my thighs. Then suddenly the music stopped, and she stepped away from me, she said thank you and asked if we would like to return to the main room, as if nothing had just happened.

I was left as stunned as I had been when I first went in.

I picked my bag up and followed Sam back into the main room, we made our way back to the same seats we were previously sat in. "Is that it then?"

Sam laughed at me "Well yes, what did you expect?"

"I don't really know, but forty pounds for five minutes, I think I'm in the wrong job!"

"Did you enjoy it?"

I smiled back at Sam "Yeah, at least, I think so, it all happened so quickly"

With that, Lexie appeared, she had gotten herself dressed again. If you can call being in her bra and briefs 'dressed' that is. "Did you enjoy the dance?"

"Yes, thank you. I hope you don't mind me asking but your eyelashes are beautiful, are they false?"

She laughed as she replied "No, they are my own"

I felt a bit bad saying that to her. "Wow, how do you get them like that?"

"I don't know, they're just like that"

I was curious to know why someone did a job like this, so I asked her.

"Because I enjoy it and I get paid for it" she smiled.

"Have you been doing it for a long time then?"

"Yes, for about twelve years"

I looked back at her in shock and began to laugh. "You must have been about twelve then!"

"No, I was eighteen, I'm thirty now"

Again, I was shocked, that lifestyle certainly agreed with her, she only looked about eighteen. I sat sipping my drink, Sam was talking to another girl, Lexie asked if I would like another dance, but I declined and said we would be heading home soon.

"Oh, that's a shame well hopefully, I will see you again sometime"

I smiled and nodded and in no time, she was gone. I finished my drink off and asked Sam if we could go. As we headed out of the club I spotted Lexie taking her next client to the room, she didn't waste much time, and there would soon be another forty pounds in her purse.

Chapter Seven

Sam was insistent on treating us to a hotel for the night after his big win at the casino. There was one not too far from where we were, so we made our way to that one. Part of me was thinking what a waste of money as I had a perfectly good bed at home, while the other part of me was quite excited at the thought of staying in a hotel. Not that I had never stayed in a hotel before, just that I had not stayed in one just for sex. And when I say just for sex, I don't mean that there was nothing between us, but as I said I had a perfectly good bed at home. Little did I know that it was to be the first of many nights stay in a hotel.

As we walked into the hotel the guy at the reception greeted us. "Can I help?"

I was a little worse for wear and I replied. "Oh yes please" I smirked at him.

"Lizzie!" Sam looked at me in a discerning way. "I'm so sorry, my girlfriend has had a little too much to drink, I wonder if you have a room for the night?"

"Certainly sir, we have a double room on the first floor"

"Yes, that will be fine thank you"

Sam signed for the room and took directions of where it was.

We locked lips the second we got through the door to the room, dragging one another's clothes off like we had never had sex with each other before. As we fell onto the bed I felt Sam's hot breath against my skin and his lips moved slowly over my body. The strong scent of his aftershave aroused me more than usual and triggered off that wanting in me. I began to think about Lexie and the dance she gave me and wondered what it would be like if we were to have our own ménage à trois.

His hand cupped my breast and his tongue teased my nipple, he fondled my other nipple with his other hand rubbing it between his finger and thumb. Spinning me over he rubbed his erection against my buttocks, gripping the cheeks of my arse with both hands, he was hard and pressing up against me.

I turned back over and kissed him, pushing him onto his back on the bed. I climbed on top and slid myself down onto him, briefly making eye contact with him as I let out a moan. With my hand flat to his chest I began to move at a faster pace, feeling him harder inside me. I began to pant, I could feel an orgasm coming. I tilted my head back and gasped loudly as it happened.

He let the last of it flood out of me and spun me around onto my back before entering me again. Slowly easing himself in before he began to gather speed. I could feel and hear his breathing as he nuzzled his head into my neck. He murmured with every thrust, and as his body stiffened I could feel his cock pulsing inside of me as he came.

He lay back on the bed and relaxed, "That was great".

I let out a sigh and agreed with him, what a night we had had.

He propped his head on his elbow and said, "I really can't believe you did that tonight"

"Did what? Had a lap dance?" I began to laugh. "No neither can I"

"No not that, I mean afterwards, you've just had a new erotic experience in your life and you ask her if her lashes are false"

We both curled up laughing. "I was curious, nothing wrong with that"

Sam kissed me, and I kissed him back eagerly. I slipped my hand between his legs and held him in my hand, he was sticky and still soft from round one, but I could feel him starting to grow at my touch. I brushed his nipple with the end of my tongue, placing my lips round it, tasting the salt of his sweat on his skin. He looked down at me and said "Hmm if this is what lap dancers do to you maybe we should go every night"

I looked back at him and replied, "I don't need a lap dancer"

He kissed me long and hard leaving my body quivering and wanting more. I felt him now, hard and ready, he spread my legs and entered me once more. I came almost instantly, a rush of pleasure flooding my body. He ignored this completely and pumped away, wanting to reach a second orgasm of his own. After what seemed like no time at all he stiffened once again and shouted out.

We lay back on the bed together and I reached for the sheet, pulling it over us to snuggle up for the night.

The next morning the day greeted me with a headache, Sam lay fast asleep next to me. I was bursting for the loo, so I headed for the bathroom, and when I came back Sam had woken.

"Morning, God, I feel rough this morning"

"Me too, I can't understand why?" We both laughed knowing full well why we felt like this.

Sam got up and went for a shower and while he was gone his phone rang, it was on silent and a number came up but no name, I answered it. "Hi Sam's phone"

A woman's voice answered. "Sorry wrong number"

She then hung up, I held the phone and rested it against my chin, wondering who it could be. I scrambled around for some paper and quickly scribbled down the number, just in case I needed to look it up. When you've been cheated on before like I have, you become a bit of a detective suspecting everything and everyone, although I'm sure this time I was wrong. I just managed to put the phone back on the bedside table before Sam walked in, he was drying his hair and had a towel wrapped around his waist. I lay on the bed with my head resting on my hands. He looked so good, I hadn't felt like this for a long time, everything felt right, we felt right.

"Come here you sexy thing"

Sam's towel dropped to the floor and he came towards me, he looked ready for action. "Hmm have you been thinking about me again?"

He laughed and said "Always"

He grabbed my head and pulled me towards him, as he entered my mouth I could feel him pulsating. I ran my tongue down the shaft of his penis, sweeping my teeth against it, his freshly showered body smelt of the sweet floral hotel shower gel. He ran his hands through my hair, wrapping it around his fingers, drawing me further down. My hands clawed at his firm buttocks, he let out a moan as I moved up and down. I looked up at him, his eyes were closed, he was lost in the moment, enjoying every minute. I paused momentarily, and he opened his warm brown eyes to look down at me.

Our eyes locked and I began to move down again ever so slowly, holding his stare. I could feel the impact of his spunk on the back of my throat as he came. His grip tightened on the length of my hair as simultaneously his cock softened. I eased away from him and he relaxed back on the bed, letting out a sigh. I got up and made my way to the bathroom.

"That was nice babe"

I looked back and smiled at him.

As I showered my mind thought back to the phone call, what if it was another woman? Someone else he'd lied to, cheated on, how many of us were they? God knows he had the opportunity, he could have a different woman in every town he visited. I stepped out of the shower and started to dry myself, where was this coming from? This was Paul who had caused me to be like this with his infidelity. It was just a wrong number that's all, a wrong number.

I went back into the room, Sam was dressed. "I'm just going to reception to settle the bill babe, I'll see you down there" He kissed me on the cheek and he was gone. I applied some lipstick that I had found in the bottom of my bag, no point in bothering that much when I was only going home, I threw my phone etc. into my bag, quickly scanned the room for anything I might have left, then I was done.

When I got downstairs Sam was pacing up and down on his phone, he didn't seem too pleased. He looked across at me and rolled his eyes, I smiled back. He was talking quietly into his phone, quieter than he usually would I thought, but I got the feeling whoever it was he was talking to was shouting. I glanced across at him and caught his eye.

"You ok?" I mouthed. He nodded in response before rolling his eyes. The person must have cut him off as he looked at his phone in disgust before he tucked it away in his inside pocket.

"Problems?"

"You could say that, it's just John at work, he's really not a problem solver. I was trying to calm him down."

I had heard him talk to his colleague John before, he obviously wasn't his favourite person today. "Oh, I see"

"Anyway, never mind I'll get it sorted, so listen I'll give you a call tomorrow night if that's ok? I'll have to pick up the slack at work and sort his problems out"

"Ok, are you off now then?"

"Yes, best get off and sort this, or it could lead to all sorts of problems"

"No problem let me know how it goes then"

"I will do babe" He bent down and gave me a lingering kiss and then made his way out of the hotel.

He didn't seem right this morning obviously work was worrying him. I called for a taxi and waited in the foyer, I once again thought about the phone call.

It was mid-morning when I got home, I made myself a coffee and sat with my feet up on the sofa. I grabbed a magazine off the coffee table in front of me. 'Pumping Iron' - I really didn't want to read that, Caroline had become so obsessed with this keep fit lark. I put it back on the table and sat back with my eyes closed thinking about the last twenty-four hours and the wrong number. I knew I was being silly, but I had to know, I went to grab my phone from my bag and rang my best friend Dawn.

"Hi, how are you?"
"I'm good thanks and you?"
"Yeah, I'm ok working hard you know, same old thing"
"But not today?"
"What?"
"You're not working today?"
"Oh, no I rang in sick"
"And are you?"
"What?"
"Sick?"
"Well yes, I mean no, not really"
"Ah, so was it a Sam day?"
"Sorry?"
"Your day today was it a Sam day"
"Oh yes, well we were out last night, and I was a bit worse for wear"
"Well I hope he's worth it"
"Yes, he is"
"I wouldn't know I've not met him yet!"
"I know don't worry you will"

I had been having the odd day off work, ringing in sick just so I could meet Sam when he was in between business meetings.

"If you say so, and how is Sam?"

"Oh, don't judge me please, I've just rung for some advice" I knew Dawn wasn't too sure about Sam, she had made that clear when I first met him, telling me that I should be careful, 'These business men are all the same you know'. But despite all that I knew she would always listen to me and knowing what I had been through with Paul she would understand my suspicions.

I began to tell Dawn about my night with Sam, and the phone call.
"So, what do you think I should do?"

"Well in view of everything you have been through its probably best for you to ring the number and ask who she is"

"But what if she won't speak? I think I would be better texting"

"Ok, well text then and see if she replies"

Dawn knew that I couldn't be messed about anymore, and that's why she worried about me so much. "I'm going to do it now, I'll text you later"

Dawn was a good friend, the best, always there for me when I needed her. She had married young and soon became a single mum, but she coped well, better than I ever could have, she was always more than organised.

I ended the call and looked around for the number. Shit where did I put it? I looked in the pocket of my coat, there was a petrol receipt but no number. Then I remembered, I think I dropped it in my bag at the bedside, yes there it was. I nervously typed the number into the phone and thought about what I could write, some time went by before I could think of what to put, should I just ask who it is? I really wasn't sure. But then I thought, why mess about? I'll just get straight to the point.

'Hi, not sure if you were a wrong number today, but if you weren't I think we should maybe meet up.'

I nervously waited for a reply, I thought it would be a while before I heard anything, so I went to the kitchen to make myself a cup of tea.

I was just putting the milk back into the fridge when I heard my phone beep. I made my way back into the living room to view the reply.

'When and where?'

Hell no, it wasn't a wrong number, she must have known Sam.

'Do you know where the Chafron Hotel is?'

'Yes, what time?'

She even knew where our hotel was, when should I meet her?

'What about seven this evening?'

'That's fine I'll see you in the lounge then at seven'

'Ok see you later, Lizzie'

I sent the message and realised I had put my name. I wasn't too sure if I should have done that, oh well it was done now.

I text Dawn back and told her what was happening, she said that at least I would get it sorted and know where I stood, whereas I felt like I had opened a can of worms.

Chapter Eight

I spent the rest of the afternoon deciding what to wear, I didn't want to look too sexy, but not too shabby either. I needed to be smart but look attractive, after all, I didn't know what I was up against. After spending the best part of an hour staring into the wardrobe I decided on a smart black pencil skirt and black top. I smoothed the skirt down with my hands whilst looking at my reflection in the mirror, 'yes, this'll do' I thought to myself. I looked like I could handle whatever was about to be thrown at me.

I got a taxi to the Chafron and arrived around six forty-five, I needed to be there first, to hopefully check her out before she spotted me. I entered the hotel and made my way through to the bar, it was quite busy, so I found myself a stool at the bar itself and waited to be served. My stomach was churning like an overloaded washing machine.

I was still waiting to be served when I felt like someone's eyes were boring into the back of me, I turned around and caught sight of a woman stood a couple of feet behind me. She was probably a similar age to me, her hair was a rich burgundy colour, she was attractive and about five foot eight. She briefly looked away then looked back at me, eyeing me up like the terminator would, capturing every inch of me, starting at my feet and working her way up until finally, we locked eyes with each other.

She moved towards my bar stool and said "You must be Lizzie" in a very 'matter of fact' manner.

"That's right, and you are?" I looked away towards the bar as I said it.

"I'm Jenny. His wife"

I looked back at this woman in front of me and my anger quickly shifted to sympathy. I recognised the hurt in her eyes as they filled with tears, and I could feel her heart breaking, after all, I had been there myself. I reached into my bag for my purse.

"Would you like a drink?"

She nodded as she blinked back the tears that welled up inside her, her hard stare had completely disappeared. I glanced around the room and wondered if we could find a seat somewhere. I looked back at her "Do you drink wine?"

"Yes, white please"

I ordered a bottle of Sauvignon blanc, I figured we would both be needing more than just a glass.

We found a quiet corner of the hotel and took to our seats, I poured us both a rather large glass of the wine and shifted awkwardly in my chair, waiting in anticipation for what I assumed would be some hard to answer questions.

"So, do you come here on a regular basis? I mean is this where he is when he's working away?"

She did that inverted commas thing with her fingers that everyone does, and her eyes began to well up again. I looked away, I suddenly felt a lot more uncomfortable.

"Look there's no point in us going over this"

"There is every point, I need to know everything"

"Oh, please you'll be telling me I'm not the first soon"

"You're not"

I felt deflated, everything he had said to me, like did he look married! Well apparently, he did because he was. It transpired that Sam had done this before but had sworn he would never do it again. Why didn't

I see this before? after what I had previously experienced with Paul I should have known better.

I first had my suspicions about Paul when he was allegedly sleeping out at a friend's place after a night out. He had never done that before, so I couldn't understand why he would be doing it now. Then one night he left his phone downstairs after he had gone to bed. I know I shouldn't have, and I knew it wouldn't end well, but I decided I had to see what was on it. I needed to know if I was right about him, and I desperately hoped I wouldn't be.

Unfortunately, my gut instinct had been right, and I found some texts from Suzanne, she was another personal fitness instructor from our school. The last text from her was to say that she could make Friday and she would be at the Thurston Hotel at the usual time. Paul had replied with 'see you there x'. I felt sick when I read it, I wanted to confront him straight away but that would be no good, there was no proof in that. I had to catch them together. I thought about going on the Friday night to catch them meeting in the hotel, but as I didn't know what time they would be meeting, I decided to wait for them coming out in the morning.

The Thurston was about ten miles out of town, so it wasn't that far away. I got to the hotel at around eight on the Saturday morning, I could see Pauls car in the car park. I looked for somewhere that I could park and not be seen, and fortunately there was a spot further back. I pulled into the spot and waited nervously, I thought about getting out of the car and confronting them both, but I wasn't sure that I would be up to that. It wasn't like I didn't know her for goodness sake, I worked with her. I tried flicking through the social media on my phone, but I couldn't even concentrate on that.

An hour passed by and as I was just about to leave the door of the hotel opened and there they were. I thought I would choke with the emotion that welled up inside me, my heart was beating like thunder, ringing in my ears. They made their way to Paul's car, he slid his hand around her waist and gave her a lingering kiss. Anger rose inside me,

I was helpless, I could never compete with her, she was as Paul would say fit, and I, well I wasn't fit. Not in comparison with her anyway. I tried to take a picture, it would be my proof, evidence, whatever you want to call it.

My eyes misted up with tears, I had been suspicious for a while but the reality of it was more painful than I could imagine. I challenged Paul about Suzanne that night when he got in and at first, he said I was crazy and that he would never do anything like that to me. It was then that I produced my evidence, the picture, it wasn't perfect, but it did the trick. He sunk into the chair and begged me for forgiveness, telling me he would never see her again, which may be quite difficult as he worked with her. Of course, I foolishly believed he would end this supposedly very short affair and I took him back.

"So, was he a good fuck?" Jenny's harsh remarks jolted me out of my thoughts. I looked up at her, blinking away the tears that filled my eyes. "Well, was he?"

I didn't know what to say.

"Does he just roll over and go to sleep after? Is it the same every time? Well, is it?"

I just wanted to get up and go, this morning I had thought he was cheating on me with another woman when in fact he was cheating on her with me.

"Look I'm sorry but this is getting us nowhere, I've got to go"

I moved to grab my bag from the table and got up, Jenny placed her hand on mine. "No, I'm sorry. Please stay, I just need to know some things"

I looked across at her and then closed my eyes to compose myself, I needed all the strength I had to stop me from crying. I sat back down and took a sip of my wine.

"How did you meet, and where?" Jenny asked.

I picked up my wine glass again and took a large gulp from it. "Look we literally bumped into each other in a pub one night, we just seemed to click with each other"

"How nice" she retorted vindictively.

"Look, I honestly had absolutely no idea he was married, if I had I would never have gone out with him, I promise you. I know what it's like to be in your position"

"Well, that's good of you, how long?"

"Not long"

"How long, a month, a year? Just give me the truth, you owe me that"

"About eight months I think"

"You think! Don't you know?"

"Ok, yes it was eight months"

She slammed her glass on the table and stood up. "I should throw this wine over you, you make me sick"

I stood up to face her and leant over the table. "Go on then! Throw the fucking wine if it makes you feel better! Hit me, do what you have to, just get it over with! I'm telling you I had no fucking idea he was married, I even asked him!"

She picked the glass up again and I waited. She finished the rest of the wine from it and sat back down, picked up the wine bottle and filled her glass, then mine. I looked at my glass and took a sip of it and as I did she said - "I was pregnant". I looked up at her, I was speechless.

She closed her eyes and more tears fell, I searched the bottom of my bag for a tissue and handed it to her as she began to sob. She looked back at me, her dark eyelashes damp with tears, and as she choked away more tears she thanked me, before holding the tissue to her mouth in an attempt to stifle her emotions. I wiped my own tears away with the back of my hand and looked down into my wine glass, nervously running my finger around the glass.

"Look, I'm sorry, I really don't know what to say"

"I lost the baby, about nine months ago" I covered my face with my hands as the guilt took hold further. "I was devastated, he said I needed to get over it and just carry on, but I couldn't, he didn't understand how I needed time to grieve"

I nodded as she explained what had happened, and I found myself holding her hand to comfort her. She explained how Sam had done this before a few years ago but swore never to do it again, then she asked me the question I'd been waiting for.

"Do you want to be with him?"

I shook my head. "No, you see I've been here myself, and I can't do it, not to you or anyone" I told Jenny about Paul and what had happened, and we sat in silence for a while.

"What about you?"

"What?"

"Do you want to stay with him?"

She pulled at the tissue in her hand and paused for a while. "No, no I don't think I do, I don't think I should"

"Neither do I, you're better than that"

For the first time through the pain she carried she smiled, I smiled back at her, she didn't deserve to be treated like that.

"I need the loo" She stood up and disappeared through the hotel. I looked around the room and wondered how it had come to this, how could I do this to someone. We had met in this very hotel, had sex in these rooms. I wish I could say made love, but I can't now, I know that it was never that. I glanced up again and I could see her making her way to the bar, she brought us back another bottle of wine.

We sat and chatted till the early hours, drinking numerous bottles of wine, plotting how we would seek revenge on Sam. From tying him up and leaving him naked somewhere, to taking all his money and running off and spending it. I don't think either of us were in any fit state to make a sensible decision on how to deal with him. We somehow managed to swop phone numbers and I said I would contact her. Jenny's taxi came first, and I was shocked when she hugged me before she left.

"Thank you, and don't forget to ring me"

"I really don't think you should be thanking me"

"I do, if you hadn't answered the phone I would still be living a lie"

I promised that I would call her tomorrow and I waved her off as her taxi disappeared out of the hotel grounds. The whole evening seemed a bit surreal, starting off like we were going to tear each other to bits and then kind of becoming some sort of friends.

The next morning, I felt dreadful and had to ring in sick again, the trouble he had caused me. I had never been one to be off work and here I was again only this time I wasn't meeting him, I was nursing a hangover because of him. As I ended the phone call I laid back down on the bed and hoped I would feel better after a couple of hours sleep.

When I woke again and looked up at my alarm clock, the digital numbers read 12.05. I'd been asleep for about four hours, I still felt rough, I needed a coffee. I made my way downstairs. As I flicked the kettle on I could hear my phone signalling to me that I had a message. I looked around the kitchen, but couldn't see it anywhere, I sauntered through to the hallway and found my handbag, and in it my phone. I had four messages and five missed calls, all from Sam, the latest one asking me to meet him that night. I sat on the sofa wondering what to do, I began to text.

"Yeah, sure what time? x"

"Our usual place at around 7 pm? x"

"Yes, look forward to it x"

"Great see u later x"

Chapter Nine

That afternoon I played through lots of different scenarios in my head of how I could tell him that I knew that he was married, and then the perfect way came to mind.

I had a long soak in the bath to try and shake my headache off, and thankfully it worked. Afterwards whilst looking for something to wear my phone rang, it was Jenny.
"Hi, how are you feeling?"
"Not too bad now, but I felt awful this morning. How about you?"
"Same here, I've not had that much to drink for ages" We both laughed. "I was just wondering has he asked you to meet him tonight?"
I paused before I answered. "Yes, he has, I wasn't going to go but I want to tell him what I think of him to his face"
Jenny was momentarily quiet. "I thought so, he said he is having to stay over as he has an early start tomorrow"
"Oh, so he thinks I'm staying out with him?"
"It sounds that way"
"Well he's in for a shock"
We chatted for a while longer and arranged to contact each other the next day. I carried on getting ready, applying my makeup as perfect as I could, a little mascara to lengthen my lashes and a touch of eyeliner to widen my eyes. I chose a deep red lipstick and ran it over my lips, pursing them together into a pout to check I hadn't missed anywhere.

I stared back at myself in the mirror. I wanted to look sexy, make him really want me. I found some stockings and matching underwear, a black lace plunging bra and a lace thong. I slipped a little black dress on and I was ready.

I arrived at the hotel just after seven, as I walked in the door I could see Sam was already stood waiting for me in the bar area. I made my way over to him.

"Hi"

He grabbed my hand and gently kissed me on the lips, I wanted to turn away, but I couldn't, I smiled. "Hi"

"I'll get you a drink"

As he waited at the bar to be served I looked across at him, his unshaven look still turned me on as much as it had when I first saw him, and I couldn't believe he had lied to me like that. As I drifted off thinking about the fun times we had shared together, I began to feel the need to be with him again, just one last time. Feeling him next to me, I needed him. Then I remembered everything Jenny had been through and our lengthy conversation last night, and I realised that I needed to stay focused. I couldn't go back now.

Sam took my hand and lead me to a secluded corner in the hotel. "You're looking exceptionally sexy tonight"

"Meaning that I don't usually look sexy?"

He caught hold of a stray strand of my hair and gently tucked it behind my ear. "No, I don't mean that. You always look sexy, it's just tonight you look extra hot".

I smiled back at him and momentarily forgot my plan of action, I bent forward and kissed him, long and hard. He smelt so good, he was wearing his usual aftershave, the scent of it teasing me once again. I felt my desire for him grow inside me.

"Shall we go up to the room?"

"You've booked a room, that was a bit presumptuous of you, wasn't it?"

He laughed. "It's what we do isn't it?"

Not for much longer I thought. I smiled up at him and patted the seat beside me. "Come and sit down for a while, let's at least finish this drink"

Normally there would have been no stopping me I would been in the room now, clothes all over the floor and wanting more. Sam placed his pint on the table and reluctantly sat beside me. "We could take our drinks to the room?"

I took a sip of wine "Yes, we could, but there's plenty of time, no rush"

He moved closer to me, placing his hand on my leg. As he kissed me I felt his hand gently slide up the inside of my leg, reaching the bare flesh above my stocking top. I gasped and broke away, trying to stop the urge to drag him to the room.

"So why didn't you pick up the phone or answer my texts today"

I could feel myself turning red as he asked the question. "I was busy, we had a meeting at work, just about Ofsted. So how was your meeting with John yesterday, did you sort it out?"

Sam turned to face me. "John?"

"Yes, you said he was having a bit of a meltdown I think. Well, something like that" I managed to spin the ball back to him, and I waited for his reply.

"Oh John, yes I managed to sort things out with him. He doesn't cope well under pressure, bless him"

The words just rolled off his tongue, I couldn't believe it, he was a natural liar. I picked my glass up and turned to him. "Maybe he's the wrong man for the job then?"

"No, he's ok, he means well, he just gets a bit panicky under pressure"

I gulped my wine down. "Can you get me another drink please, I just need the loo" I made my way to the toilet, my mind racing trying to think how I was going to handle this.

The toilets were empty, I stared at myself in the mirror as I reapplied my lipstick, trying to think of a way out of this relationship. I really must stay strong, and not be taken in by him.

When I got back my wine was waiting for me on the table, Sam was texting someone.

"Anyone I know?"

He looked up at me startled. "No, just someone from work"

"John?"

"No, look, are you ok?"

"Me? Yes, why?"

"You just seem a bit edgy"

"I'm fine, just a bit tired. I've had a busy day"

"Bit like me then" He reached forward and took another large swig of his drink.

I squeezed his knee as I sat down, Sam slipped his phone into his inside pocket. "Maybe we should finish these drinks and call it a night?"

"Hey, come on Lizzie, I've got us a room remember" He leant towards me again, nuzzling his head into my neck. I could feel his soft lips brushing against me, as his over grown stubble tickled me. I wanted him so much. We began to kiss, his hand strayed, finding its way up my dress. I was already wet for him. He grabbed my hand. "Come on"

I got up from the chair, reaching for my bag. "Can we take a bottle of wine up?"

"Sure, why not, I'll order some when we get back to the room"

As we made our way to the room we stopped on the way in the corridor and began to kiss.

"You know how much you turn me on don't you Lizzie?" I smiled back at him, I wasn't sure to be fair, but I knew that he turned me on.

We eventually made it up to the room, I hardly had time to kick my shoes off before we had locked together. As we pressed up to each other I could feel that he was hard and ready for me. I helped Sam slip his jacket off, he kissed me again then turned me around. He guided me towards the foot of the bed, bending me over it he hitched my dress up, and slipped my thong down. As I waited I wondered what was happening, I looked behind me and just caught sight of Sam easing his pants down. I turned away just as he entered me and shrieked with excitement, the rhythmic motion had me yearning for more.

As I lay on the bed afterwards, Sam lay beside me snoring, just as Jenny had said he did, he'd rolled over and gone to sleep. A wave of guilt flowed over me, what had I done? I promised Jenny that I would end it with Sam tonight and here I was laid next to him in the afterglow. I couldn't hurt Jenny anymore and I didn't feel I could trick Sam any longer into thinking everything was ok between us. I eased myself off the bed as quietly as I could and got dressed. I gently kissed his soft lips for one last time and he stirred momentarily.
"Where are you going babe?"
"I'm just nipping down stairs for that bottle of wine"
He pushed his face into his pillow and said. "Ring room service, they'll bring us one"
"No, it's fine I won't be long" I slipped my shoes on and made my way out of the room, gently closing the door. I leant up against the door, realising it would be the last time I would see him. Blinking away the tears I made my way back to the reception. "Can I order a taxi please?"
"Certainly, when for?"
"Now please"
He picked up the phone and booked me a taxi, it wasn't very long before it arrived outside.

I was only in the taxi a few minutes when my phone rang, it made me jump, it was Sam. The taxi driver asked if I was ok, I could only manage a brief 'yes thanks' in response. I switched my phone onto silent and dropped it back into my bag. I could feel it vibrating all the way home.
When I reached home I had ten missed calls from Sam, and four texts which read.

Pamela Christine

'I'm waiting, where are you?'

'I'm not bothered about the wine just come back'

I held the phone to my chest, tears stung my eyes, what was I doing? Not only was I hurting myself, but I had let jenny down too. I glanced down at my phone to read the other messages.

'Are we playing games tonight?'

'Where are you?'

I ignored them all. I wanted to be with him but couldn't go through with it after everything that I had been through with Paul, especially knowing that I would be hurting Jenny as well. I couldn't do that to her, I had already gone too far this evening.

Chapter Ten

My mind drifted back to a time when I was out shopping with Paul, we had been in several shops, had some lunch to refuel and then hit some more. There were some brilliant sales on and I couldn't resist a bargain. We were in one of the boutiques on the high street and I had an arm full of clothes, Paul was just following me around playing with his mobile phone, carrying all the bags from the previous shops we'd been in.

"I'm just going to try these on, I won't be long"

"Ok" He muttered, he sat down on one of the chairs outside as I disappeared into one of the fitting rooms, unable to tear his eyes from his phone. I tried the first dress on, God that was a no, I looked awful in it. I picked up the next one, now this was more like it I thought. Black lace from top to bottom, hem just above the knee, and it clung to me in all the right places, enhancing my breasts. It made me feel quite sexy, and most importantly, I knew Paul would love it. So that would go on the keep pile. I had a few more items to try on, a couple of pairs of jeans and some tops to go with them, I had been in there ages. I heard my phone bleep, I knew it would be Paul asking where I was, I quickly took the jeans off and checked. As I'd suspected it was Paul.

'I'm leaving'

Bless him, he must have got bored.

Pamela Christine

'*Ok, where shall I meet you?*'

A message came straight back.

'*I'm leaving*'

'*Yes, I get that where do you want to meet? I won't be long now.*'

He didn't reply, he never did have much patience. I decided to leave the other items and head for the tills with the black lace dress, he will love it.

As I came out of the shop Paul was nowhere to be seen. I hated it when he did this, just goes off and I have to spend ages looking for him. I decided to ring him and find out where he was, so I wasn't wasting too much time searching for him. It went straight to answer phone so I left him a message, he would get straight back to me like he always did.

I stayed close to the shops we had been in, but he didn't ring back, I could only assume his battery had gone dead, after all, he had been on his phone most of the day. I decided to go on ahead to the car park figuring he was probably waiting there for me, however when I arrived there he was nowhere to be seen and I couldn't find our car either. I think I had got myself into such a state that I couldn't remember where it was. I asked the car park attendant to help me to try and find it and he did - try that is. We walked up and down several times, but it wasn't there. I wondered if Paul had been called to an emergency, I knew his mum hadn't been in the best of health lately. I realised I was going to have to give up and went back into the centre to catch the bus.

When I eventually reached home at about five thirty, the car was on the drive, meaning Paul must be inside. I tried the door handle, but it was locked, I knocked and searched for my keys in the meantime. Nobody came and answered so when I eventually found them I let myself in.

"Paul?" I called his name from the hallway but there was no answer. I threw my keys on the hall table and made my way through the house. I kept shouting, but he wasn't there. How strange... I wondered where he could be?

I made my way back to the kitchen and flicked the kettle on, my bags filled with bargains bought earlier in the day lay on the table, along with a hand-written note and the keys to my car. I picked it up and began to read, my hands beginning to shake the further I read.

Lizzie

I really can't do this anymore, I've realised I want to be with Suzanne. She said I can move in with her so I'm going.

I know its short notice but there's no point in us carrying on like this, it's best to end it now. For the past few weeks I have tried to put Suzanne out of my mind, but I can't. You probably think I'm a coward doing it this way, and maybe I am, but either way it must be done.

I'll pop for the rest of my stuff sometime in the week.

Paul

I ran outside to see if his car was in the garage and my worst fears were confirmed. It was gone. We had gone out in mine that morning as it was already on the drive.

What the hell was he playing at? I forgave him, took him back, tried to forget everything he had done, and most of all I continued to love him despite everything. I made my way back into the kitchen, my heart was breaking once again as I screwed up the letter and threw it across the room, screaming out in anger. Only a couple of hours ago we were shopping together, we'd had lunch, and everything seemed normal. I rang my friend Dawn and sobbed down the phone to her, she was great with me and not once did she say, 'I told you so'.

I got over the weekend and rang work on the Monday morning to explain that my husband once again had taken off with Suzanne their other fitness instructor. I wanted to blame them for employing her, but I knew that was just senseless. I told them I couldn't face work now and that I was going to see my doctor. To be fair to the school they were really good with me and said they understood.

I spent the rest of the day clearing Paul's wardrobe out, it was my plan to throw his clothes out on the street, but I thought why show myself up for him? In the end I just threw his clothes into bin bags and put them in the garage, which I thought was quite civilised of me.

And that was that really, I insisted eventually that we sold the house. I didn't want another woman making new memories in the house that we had shared together, and the rest as they say, is history.

It was just after midnight and my phone beeped, it was Jenny.

'Are you back home?'

I replied straight away. *'Yes'*

'Can I ring you?'

I wasn't sure that I had the courage to speak to her, but after thinking about it for a few minutes I decided to call her.
"Hi"
"Well, how did it go, did you tell him?"
"No, I couldn't"
"Because you want to be with him?"
"No not at all, I don't want to be with him" I was glad she couldn't see me, she would have seen straight through me. I could feel my face flushing, through both lies and embarrassment.

"Did he want you to go back to his room?" Jenny asked. "Lizzie are you there?"

"Yes, I'm here"

"Did you kiss?"

"Look Jenny I'm going to have to go. I'm at work in the morning and I can't be off again, I'll ring you tomorrow"

"If you are going to be with him and staying with him tonight, I really don't think there is any point in us contacting each other again"

"But I'm not, I'm at home"

"If you say so"

"I do, and I am, I have no cause to lie to you"

There was an awkward silence between us, and then Jenny said. "Very well I'll ring or text you when he's next staying over somewhere and we can meet here if you want? Although he probably won't be staying away as much now"

"I'm sure he will he wasn't always with me you know"

With that Jenny said. "I'll ring you" And she put the phone down.

We left it that Jenny would ring me when he was next away, but I didn't hear from her again. I think she must have sensed something. Sam on the other hand, was ringing me every day, sometimes three or four times. He even sat outside the house one night, but I didn't go out and see him. Caroline was going mad saying that I should at least speak to him, but I didn't want to, I didn't trust myself, or the fact that he could wrap me round his little finger. I couldn't risk it.

Chapter Eleven

The following week the calls started to die down, Sam only rang a couple of times and then stopped bothering. I was three weeks away from half term and couldn't wait, I was tempted to go on holiday somewhere, even if I had to go by myself. I didn't care, I just needed to get away. I had a look at some deals online but I wasn't sure what I was doing, so I decided I'd have to go into town to the travel agents the next day.

That same evening, I gave Dawn a ring to see if she fancied going out for a drink, it took a while for her to negotiate a babysitter but about half an hour later she rang me back to say we were on. We met at one of the popular bars in the town, she hadn't been out for a while and was well and truly ready to let her hair down. We started on the shots, then moved onto the flavoured gin's, as we drank I told her the full story about Sam and Jenny, and what a mess the whole thing was.

"To be honest, all I want to do right now is go on holiday and forget about it all" I sighed.

"So, why don't you?"

"Well for a start I have no one to go with, and secondly… well there is no secondly"

"So why don't we go together? I haven't been away for ages!" she grinned, I could see she was already getting excited about the prospect of a little sunshine.

"Would you come? What about the kid's?"

"I'll ask Mum and Dad if they would mind watching them for me"

"Great, well I was going to go and book something tomorrow"

"Well can you leave it until the afternoon? And I'll get hold of Mum in the morning"

"I don't see why not!" I began to get excited with her.

"Where are you thinking of going?"

"Not sure really, just somewhere with a cheap deal"

"Well I have some money from my divorce settlement, not much but I will definitely get a cheap holiday out of it" the smile on her face getting bigger by the second.

"That's great Dawn, I'll meet you in town tomorrow afternoon" I smiled back at her, I really was pleased she'd be coming away with me, it'd do us both a world of good.

We danced the night away in the pubs and talked about what we would do whilst we were away, I just hoped Dawn's mum would have her kids.

The next day we met and spent a good hour or so in the travel agents before finally booking the holiday. We ended up going with Portugal, I had never been abroad before, so it would be a whole new experience.

The time flew by and it wasn't too long before we were boarding the plane, we ordered some wine and said we would start as we mean to go on, we didn't eat much and drank ourselves to sleep. We woke up groggy as we landed, feeling slightly worse for wear, which wasn't helped much as we stepped off the plane and was met by a wall of intense heat. All I needed was a bit of fresh air to, but it was stiflingly hot. I looked around at the scenery, you could see the local village beyond the runway and the mountains behind the main building of the airport. I wondered what I had done, the place looked tired and barren. In all honesty, I thought I had entered a war zone, nothing looked finished. We headed into the terminal, Dawn's case was circling on the carousel as we arrived at it, so she took it went off to grab us some bottled water, then quickly freshen herself up in the toilets. I waited for my case to appear on the carousel, as one by one everyone else's started to disappear. I was hoping that my case wouldn't be the last one off, then as if by magic there she was, my old faithful. She had seen better days, many happy holidays with Mum and Dad in Wales, and of course there was Gretna with Paul. I pulled it from the conveyer belt quickly and head off to meet up with Dawn.

We arrived at our apartment mid-afternoon, it was nice, spacious and clean. We had a nice balcony with plenty of room and a table with a couple of chairs that I could see us having pre-evening drinks on. As soon as we dropped our bags off I wanted to hit a bar for refreshment, but Dawn wanted to ring her mum to check on the kids. I told her I was going for a walk and that I would catch up with her later.

I left the complex and made my way over to the sea, removed my shoes and strolled along the sandy beach at the water's edge. It was clean and unspoilt, the gentle waves were lapping at my toes, feeling cold but refreshing in the heat. I am such a wimp, I always was, always the last one in the swimming pool as a child on holiday. That was until Dad threw me in and I had to sink or swim, not the best way to learn how to swim.

Two bronzed guys' ran past me racing one another along the beach, rather them than me in this heat, I thought. The sea felt nice now that I was used to it, it was always ok when you got used to it. I wandered along for a while thinking about the last few weeks and what a mess it all was, my mind drifted back to happier times with Paul. He made me feel good, we were right for each other, how did we end up like this? I could feel tears welling up inside me, but before my mind wandered any further I was snapped back to reality by a voice next to me asking "Would you like to go on the banana boat?"

I looked up and stared at the hunk stood before me, his skin was tanned from the sun, glistening with a slight sweat from being out on the beach all day, dark almost black hair and a cheeky smile.

"Erm, no thank you, I'll give it a miss I think" I blushed.

He continued to try and persuade me as I walked away, I decided what I needed right now was a sleep, so I made my way back to the apartment.

When I got back the door to the apartment was propped open with one of Dawns flipflops and Dawn was asleep on one of the beds. I was going to put my clothes away in the wardrobe, but I couldn't be bothered, I just flopped on to the bed and drifted off to sleep.

The first couple of days we were just finding our feet, trying to find our way around the resort, we got quite friendly with the barmen and usually managed to get extra shots from them. Although I don't believe we were special or anything, as all the single girls got shots and the odd free drink. Dawn had taken a shine to Mateo the barman at the bar in our apartments. I did try to warn her that he was a bit of a lady's man, but she didn't seem to care.

Dawn was an attractive woman, she used to have long blonde hair when we first started hanging around together, which was getting on for eight or nine years ago. She used to tease the men with it, twirling it around her finger while looking across at them. When she had the kids, she had it all cut off, she said she didn't have time to mess with it but she still looked stunning. She used to have the men flocking round her and judging by the attention she was receiving on this holiday nothing much had changed.

We were downing the shots, and hammering the cocktail menu, it was helping me forget what a mess my life was at the moment. Dawn persuaded me to sit down with her and Mateo, he had a friend with him, but he spoke very little English, so things weren't going so well. I told Dawn I was going to the bar and that I would see her later. I had to go, I was beginning to feel awkward in the situation and even though Mateo had brought his friend I still felt like a bit of a gooseberry.

"Wait!" Dawn shouted across to me as I got up to leave the table, she leaned forward and grabbed my hand. "Will you be ok?"

"Of course, I'll be fine, I'm a big girl you know" I smiled across at her and Mateo.

"I know but I don't want to bail out on you"

"You're not, I'm bailing out on you"

Dawn lent forward and kissed me on the cheek. "See you later Hun"

I kissed her back on the cheek and said "Yeah take care, don't do anything I wouldn't do"

She looked across at me and winked. "All the scope in the world then"

As I made my way through the club I pushed past a group of people allegedly dancing and I looked for an empty space at the bar. There was one empty stool at the bar and I inelegantly sat myself on it. The alcohol was beginning to take a hold on me, I sat with my elbows on the bar and my head in my hands. As I gazed through the gaps in my fingers I pondered over what I should have to drink next.

"Tequila Lizzie?" Miguel the barman shouted.

"Yeah, Tequila" I answered as I raised my hand in the air, quickly bringing it down to steady my head with my hands. "Miguel, Miguel" I shouted. He looked up and nodded his head as if responding to me.

"Forget it Miguel, I'll just have water"

"Water?"

"Yes water…Please" God what was I doing? And just for the sake of a man.

The water was placed on the bar in front of me, and a frozen glass with a slice of lemon in it. I eventually managed to unscrew the lid of the bottle and poured the water into the glass. Everything was a bit fuzzy, I caught a glimpse of myself in the mirror behind the bar, not a pretty sight. I turned away in disgust.

I sipped the water slowly, hoping the room will soon stop spinning. Leaning my head against my hand on the bar, I stared into the room looking for Dawn. She must be long gone, I thought, I can't see her anywhere, she will be tucked up with Mateo now. I look around the room at everyone making out one way or another, or should I say hoping to. I wonder if there are any true long-term relationships out there.

I reach for another sip of my water to try and clear the mist clouding up my eyes. A young woman squeezes into my corner of the bar.

Through my distorted vision I can only make out that she has blonde hair. I try to concentrate a little more on my vision and I establish that it definitely isn't Dawn, because this woman has really short hair. I notice she has a pair of sunglasses on her head that clearly cost more than the five-euro ones that I recently bought. She orders a rum and coke and leans her back towards the bar, casually resting her elbows on it.

She glances towards me - "Hi" – she smiles, a big genuine smile, flashing teeth that probably cost as much as the sunglasses. I turn around to see who she is speaking to, she laughs and as I look back at her she says. "I said Hi…" She spoke with an American accent.

"Oh, sorry, were you speaking to me?" I reply, slurring my words.

"I sure was… Allie" She holds her hand out for me to shake.

As I try to pull myself together I grab her hand and say. "Lizzie"

She grips my hand so tightly I feel like I am going to be dragged off my stool. "Wow strong hand shake"

"Gee I'm sorry, sometimes I don't know my own strength"

I shuffle further back onto my stool, I take another large gulp of my water in an effort to sober myself up. She leans back against the bar and looks around the room. "So, are you here on holiday?" She asks.

"Yes, just a week, how about you?"

"Yeah, I'm just here for a couple of days, I had some business to attend to here, so I thought I would give myself some time off."

"So, what do you do?" I ask as I lean towards the bar and grab what's left of my water.

"I'm a sex therapist"

It takes everything I have to stop myself from choking on my drink, she obviously noticed as she laughed in my direction. "Really? How interesting"

The room was beginning to spin again, and I was feeling a bit nauseous. "Will you excuse me a moment?" I place my empty glass on the bar and make my way into the crowd, desperately searching for the toilets or a way out, either would do right now.

Finally, I see a WC sign. I head for the door and dash into a cubicle where I proceed to eject the whole of my stomach contents from that day, retching but wanting to try and hold on to it, I hate being sick. Just when I think I'm finished I start again. I could do with some water, I consider trying to get to the sink but as I do I start again, luckily this time there is not much to bring up.

"Lizzie are you in here?"

I grab some toilet paper and wipe it against my mouth before I answer yes. I hear Allie trying the other two cubicles before she finds me in the third. She is standing there like my saviour, with an ice-cold bottle of water in her hand. I sink onto the toilet seat as she hands me the water with the lid already removed, I gulp it down.

"Hey slow down or you'll bring it all back up again"

I think that ship had already sailed, I shake my head, take another mouthful, swill it round my vomit lined mouth, stand up and spit it in the toilet. "Never again"

"Ha, if only I had a dollar for every time I had said that, I would be rich"

I had kind of thought she already was but maybe I was wrong. Allie left the cubical and came back with a damp paper towel and placed it over my forehead. "This might help"

I felt the cold on my forehead as it soaked the beads of sweat up. I looked up at Allie and just managed to say I'm sorry before I started to wretch again. I spun around to face the toilet. I felt Allie's hand on my back, rubbing gently.

"Hey, its fine we've all been here"

Hmm I thought, some more than others, and me a lot more than I wanted to of late.

"Do you fancy some fresh air Lizzie?"

I nodded back to Allie, she helped me out of the cubicle and I made my way to the sink. I washed my hands, splashed my vomit stained face with cold water and we made our way out. As the fresh air hit me I began to feel nauseous again. I unscrewed the water bottle and took a large gulp from it.

"You ok?" Allie asked.

"Yes I'm -" And with that I was sick again. "I think I'll be fine now" I was feeling quite dizzy and just wanted to sit down. "I could just do to sit down actually"

"Look my apartment isn't too far from here, would you like to come back for a coffee?"

"Yes, I will if you don't mind"

I struggled to focus and tried to concentrate on staying upright, it was then that I realised that Allie was probably the one keeping me up.

Chapter Twelve

We were soon at Allie's apartment and I was grateful that it was on the ground floor. She opened the door and I stumbled inside.

"Would you like a coffee?"

"Yes, black please"

I don't remember speaking much more than that, and a few minutes later Allie was prompting me to sit up, I think I must have nodded off. I remember shuffling further up the bed and resting my back against the wall. Allie guided my hand to the cup, I tightly clasped my fingers around the handle.

"I've added some cold water, so you can drink it now"

I nodded and smiled and began to sip the coffee. I was about half way down the cup when I felt the urge to be sick again. Allie must have noticed as she grabbed the cup from me and guided me straight to the bathroom. I pushed the door closed behind me and just made it to the toilet as I heaved, nothing but a small amount of my coffee came up. This was not good, I had to sober myself up, if my head would just stop this insane spinning I would feel better.

"Are you ok in there?" I could hear Allie shout.

"Yes, I'm fine thank you" I turned around and sat on the loo, with my head in my hands I was hot and sweating. I could feel the vomit making its way back up towards my throat. I spun around as it hit the toilet, bile, that's all that was left. I stood in front of the sink and stared at myself in the mirror, my golden tan had disappeared, my smeared eyeliner formed my panda eyes. With my grey complexion I looked good enough for the lead role in a horror movie.

I sat back on the loo, I needed to sober up and go back into the room. I tried pull myself together, I was beginning to feel better, I think I could face that coffee now. I quickly pulled my jeans up and returned to the sink, splashing myself with some water. I grabbed some toilet paper and wiped the dark smears from under my eyes. Well I didn't look great, but I looked a bit better, I opened the door and entered the room.

"You okay?" Allie was laid on the bed with her phone in her hand.

"Erm yes thanks, a lot better now, could I trouble you for another coffee please?"

"Sure, black again?"

"Yes please" I was more in focus now, I slipped my shoes off and sat down on the bed, resting my back against the wall. I looked around the room, it was very similar to ours, items of clothing strewn around, Allie must have noticed me looking.

"Sorry about the mess, I'm not the tidiest of people"

I laughed. "Its fine neither are we"

"We?"

"Dawn and me, she's my best friend, we came away together"

Allie handed me a second coffee and sat beside me. "Oh, I see, where is she then?"

"I think she left before I met you, look I'm sorry about earlier I was really out of it, I'd been drinking since this afternoon"

"Its fine really, don't worry" she smiled.

I began to tell her my life story, well the later part of my life, the bit where men were involved. She listened tentatively, from my time with Paul right up to my time with Sam and how I wished I hadn't become involved in that one.

"So, you see I've had a bit of a rough ride lately"

"Hey, haven't we all!"

A moment of silence fell in the room, I took a sip of my coffee then asked. "So how about you, I bet you have a few tales being a sex therapist?"

Allie began to laugh. "Gee I'm sorry, I'm not really a sex therapist, I just love the shocked look on people's faces when I say it, and it can be a good conversation starter. Well... that's if the person you're talking to doesn't start throwing up"

We both start laughing.

"Oh, I'm so sorry about that"

Allie put her arm around my shoulder. "Look you've had a tough time lately, it's understandable"

She was right I had had a bad time, and I'd had enough, I took another sip from my coffee which was now cold.

"I've had a bit of a rough ride too, but I gave up men a long time ago, best thing I ever did"

I made eye contact with Allie. "When you say you gave up men, do you mean...?"

"Are you asking if I am a lesbian? And should we even be labelling who we fancy, like or love in life? Surely it doesn't matter?"

For the first time since I met Allie I had got a flush of colour back into my cheeks, but this was a flush of embarrassment. I had to admit she was right, we shouldn't label people, despite being a teacher who should be politically correct I was quite bad at labelling people. But if truth be known I think most of us are.

"So, did you have a bad relationship is that why you...?" I paused to try and think of the correct way to say this. Allie saved me by stepping in.

"I've had more than one, I've had several"

"So, a bit like me then?"

Allie's arm relaxed around me and her hand was resting against my breast, I wasn't sure if I felt awkward or not by it. Allie told me about Conner a guy she started seeing in high school, thought he was going to be her forever guy, but he turned out to be a liar and a cheat. We talked till the sun rose, it was only then that I noticed the sound of the waves. I got up to look out from the balcony, Allie's apartment overlooked the beach, it was a beautiful view. I glanced down at my watch and saw that it was 6am.

"I really should go"

"Okay"

As I got to the door, I turned around and gave Allie a kiss on the cheek. "Thank you for looking after me"

"No problem, thank you for not judging"

I looked back at her and said. "I may not always have the right words, but I never judge"

"Good, you know… you can't knock it till you've tried it"

She winked at me cupped my face in her hands and kissed me quickly on the lips.

I was back at my apartment in no time, I got to the door and searched for my key, then I remembered that Dawn had it. Oh well, I would have to knock and wake her up. I banged loudly on the door - nothing - no reply, no movement. I began to shout and knock simultaneously, and that proved to be enough to rouse her as she came and answered the door.

"God, you look worse than me, what time did you get in?"

"Well a lot earlier than you because I thought you would be back"

"Sorry, we got chatting and I didn't realise what time it was"

Dawn climbed back into bed and wrapped the sheet back around her, the air conditioning gave the room a bit of a chill. "We?! Oh right! So, come on, get the kettle on and tell me, what's he like? You obviously did the deed seeing as you stayed out all night!"

I put the kettle on and began to prepare the coffee, I didn't know what to say to Dawn, if I told her I was with Allie all night she wouldn't believe me and would be nagging me for the rest of the holiday about who it really was. I poured the freshly boiled water into our mugs and found myself telling her all about my night.

"Well, after I left you I was just on my way out when I bumped into this guy"

"Go on, what's his name?"

I crawled onto my bed clutching my coffee and carried on. "His name… he's called John I think"

"You think!"

"Well I was very drunk remember! Anyway, he insisted on buying me a drink and to be honest I don't really remember much about that part of the evening" Which wasn't too far from the truth, as I was in quite a bad way. I then told Dawn how we had had mad sex all night, she was lapping it up and to be honest I didn't know that I had such a good imagination, if only she knew the truth.

"So, are you seeing him again?"

"Hell no, it was just a one-night thing,"

"Aww that's a shame"

"No, its fine I'm happy as I am, thank you" I took a sip from my coffee and hoped that Dawn wouldn't quiz me further about the night that never happened.

We continued to swap titbits from our night for a little while longer before deciding to take a trip into the town for some lunch, and a bit of retail therapy. It was a beautiful day, the baking hot sun beaming down as bright as ever, the air had that unmistakable seaside scent of salt water and the smell of Portuguese cuisine lingered, trying to entice us into one of the many restaurants we passed. As we wandered round the busy streets I began to wonder how Allie was, I really shouldn't have just left like that.

"So, should I buy them, or do you think they will fall apart when I get home?"

I hadn't realised Dawn had been talking to me, she was trying some shoes on. "Erm yes they look great, get them" I ran my fingers along the items of clothing hanging on the rail while I waited for Dawn to pay for the shoes.

"Come on then let's go, let's go get some lunch and a drink" Dawn linked her arm in mine and we headed for the nearest bar, I looked down at my watch and realised it was only eleven thirty.

"It's a bit early isn't it?"
"For lunch or a drink?"
"Well to be honest both"
"Oh, come on Lizzie, by the time they have served us it it'll be lunchtime and besides were on holiday! I'm going to have a cocktail"

We stopped at the next bar and sat outside, the waitress came and took our order. I ordered a Pina colada, I don't know why, it was the last thing I wanted after last night, I guess I was just trying to humour Dawn. Our drinks arrived in no time and we chatted about our day so far, then not long after that our food arrived, but I was not in the mood for eating. I found myself just pushing pieces of it around my plate with my fork.

"So, what's wrong then?" Dawn asked.
"Nothing I'm fine"
"Oh, come on, you're very quiet and you haven't touched your food, don't forget I know you"
"I'm fine, just a bit hungover and tired that's all"
"I'm not surprised, staying up all night, but the question is was he worth it?"
I looked up at her and smiled. "Yes definitely"
"Well then you can't have it all ways"
We both smiled at each other, and I took a guilty sip from my cocktail. Dawn kept asking me about my non-existent guy.
"Look do you mind if we drop the subject, anyway what about you and Mateo?" With that it was like I had opened the floodgates, Dawn began to give me all the gory details and I was trying to look interested.
"Well hi! How's it going?" a voice asked from the side of our table.
Dawn stopped in her tracks and looked up, holding her hand above her eyes to shield the sun. Allie stood in front of me with white shorts and a black t-shirt, and her very expensive sun glasses balanced on her head.
"Oh... hi" I said as I felt myself blush.
"I thought you would still be catching Z's after last night"

I could see Dawn was looking puzzled at what Allie had said. I interrupted quickly before she could comment, leaving her mouth slightly ajar. "Dawn this is Allie, I got chatting to her in the club last night"

Dawn took a sip of her cocktail. "Oh right, for a minute I thought you were going to tell me this was who you really spent the night with"

I laughed awkwardly. "Oh no we just chatted for a while, look Dawn I think we best be heading back"

"Ok, sorry about this Allie, she's tired you see, she's been up with some fella all night"

"It's cool, no problem"

I looked up at Allie, I could tell by the look on her face things were far from cool. Dawn got up from her seat. "Well best get off, sorry it was short and sweet, might get to see you another time"

"Hey, no problem, and yeah... who knows"

I moved away from the table, not daring to look back. Dawn linked her arm in mine and we walked through the streets.

"She seems nice, how did you meet her?"

"Like I said, I bumped into her in the club, we just had a quick chat"

"Well there's a lot of that going on lately"

"Lot of what?"

"Bumping into people, that's how you met John didn't you?"

I looked at Dawn. "Oh yes, yes I did"

Chapter Thirteen

I just wanted to get back to the apartment, I felt so bad lying about Allie. When we got back, Dawn suggested grabbing our towels and finding a sunbed round the pool. I agreed, I had a quick shower, slipped on my bikini and grabbed a bag to carry my book and towel.

We headed to the pool, I found myself a sunbed and I tried to settle down with my book. As much as I tried I couldn't get Allie out of my head, she had been so good to me and I had let her down. I didn't even know why, what was wrong with me?

Dawn soon jolted me out of my thoughts. "Are you coming in the pool? I need to cool down"

"No, no I won't thank you, I'm going to go for a walk." I wrapped my sarong around my waist. "Dawn, would you mind taking my bag back to the room when you go please?"

Dawn jumped into the pool and called back as she wiped the water from her face and smoothed her wet hair back with her hands. "No problem see you later"

I made my way through the sunbeds, through the hotel gates and on to the main road. As I walked along the front I tried to remember where Allie's apartment was, but the only thing I could remember was that it was overlooking the beach. I walked along for a while, hoping that I would see something familiar. I remembered that there was a gift shop on the corner of the street that I came out of this morning when I left Allie's. I walked a little further and there it was, I turned down the street past the gift shop, and as I got a little further down I could see the apartments. I made my way to Allie's and paused for a while, wondering what I was going to say to her, and in all honesty, I didn't know. I knocked on the door and waited. It wasn't long before the door opened, and Allie was stood in front of me. She looked a little surprised to see me standing there, and for a moment she didn't say anything.

"Come in" She swung her arm as if she was taking a bow and stepped back to clear the way, I nervously looked towards her.

"Hi"

"Would you like a tea, coffee? Oh, wait a minute I remember coffee, black" She made her way over to the work surface and put the kettle on.

I anxiously stepped into the apartment, holding my hands close to my chest, fiddling with the gold signet ring my mother had bought me for my eighteenth. The balcony doors were open and there was a warm breeze blowing in from the sea. "Allie I just wanted to -"

Allie interrupted me. "So how was lunch?" She poured the boiled water into the cup and stirred it vigorously.

"It was ok, I wasn't really hungry. I just went to please Dawn really, but can I just -"

She interrupted me again. "And John? That was his name wasn't it? How's he, have you seen him today?" Allie grabbed her coffee and sunk onto the bed.

"Look Allie, that's what I've come about. I'm really sorry about that"

"Sorry that you felt awkward when I turned up? Or sorry that you couldn't get away from me quick enough?"

"Allie, I was just so surprised to see you, I didn't know what to say"

"I could tell that, hi, would have been nice. Do you know I never had you down as homophobic!"

"Because I'm not, I have plenty of gay friends and I did say hi"

"Only just. So, you've never spent the night at their house? Is that what you're saying?"

"What are you talking about? Yes, well of course I have," I slumped on to the end of the bed and held my head in my hands.

"I didn't even try it on with you, we were just two people chatting"

"I know, I'm sorry, I shouldn't have behaved like that today. Dawn asked me where I had been all night and I thought it would be easier just to say I had met someone, and Dawn assumed that I was with a guy and we had…" I paused for a moment.

"Been at it all night, yeah I get the picture, thank god you never told her that you spent the night with a lesbian" Allie got up from the bed, glared at me and threw the rest of her coffee down the sink. "Lizzie, I helped you, for Christ sakes if I had wanted you I could have had you at any time, you were wasted"

"Yes, I know and that's why I have come here, I just wanted to apologise."

"You hid me from your friend like some dirty secret, and for what? Like I said, we didn't even do anything"

"Allie please, at least let me apologise"

Allie walked out onto the balcony, gripping the handrail tightly she leaned forward, and I could see her shoulders rise as she took a deep breath. I followed her out and placed my hand over hers. She turned to me. "Look I'm sorry for the out pour, and sounding like a spoilt brat, but if there is one thing I can't stand its being in some one's company, who I kinda got on well with, then finding out she is just like the rest. I'm not asking you to marry me, for Christ's sake I don't even want a relationship with you. I just wanted your company that's all, I just wanted to -"

Before Allie could speak anymore, I put my finger over her lips, cupped her face in my hands and kissed her. I broke away and she leant forward and kissed me back. Her soft lips made me tingle, sending an aching down below, wanting more of her. We continued to kiss passionately, the ache, tingle or whatever you want to call it, increased. Her hand gently caressed my breast over my bikini, I pulled away. "Sorry I can't do this"

Allie pulled me back into her arms and kissed me hard. We were still kissing when she backed in to the apartment, pulling me towards her as she did. When her legs contacted with the bed, she fell onto it, dragging me with her. Our lips were still locked together, she felt like silk and smelt so sweet. I broke away for some air and gently traced my finger over her face, she smiled back at me. I softly kissed the nape of her neck, she murmured as I did. Then suddenly she clawed at my clothes like a sex starved feline, searching for the tie to my sarong, pulling at it till it came apart. In return I pulled at Allie's t-shirt till it was released from inside her tight white shorts. As I pulled it over her head I could feel her soft warm skin brushing against mine.

I held her close to me, my hand traced the arch in her back to the base of her thick blonde hair. Running my fingers through it I gripped it, as I pulled her towards me and kissed her passionately. I felt her hand slip underneath my bikini top, my breath was taken as she finally touched my breast. Allie sat astride me, I searched for the clasp of her bra and unclipped it, as the straps fell from her shoulders to reveal her breasts, I felt an extra warmth of excitement flow through me, my lips brushed against them. I pushed myself up on the bed, so our lips could meet again, we kissed briefly, and she pushed me back down. As she came towards me our breasts made contact, sending another surge of excitement through me. Her hand searched for the inside of my bikini pants, I was so wet and longing for her. I cried out as her fingers entered me, and as she went deeper I could feel the numbness of the orgasm that was about to engulf me. The rush of pleasure gathered pace and ran through my body. As I cried out she laughed playfully, I opened my eyes and looked up at her.

"What's so funny about me?"

"Not so much funny, but cute"

I began to laugh, we laid together on the bed. I thought about the last time I had laid in Sam's arm's like this, as I did I realised it really didn't matter whose arms you were laid in, male or female. All that mattered was that you were happy at that moment in time, and I was for that moment very happy.

Not long after I headed back to my apartment, Allie and I exchanged numbers and promised to keep in touch. I liked Allie, she had seen me through a tough night, she showed me a fresh way to enjoy sex and most of all she taught me never to label anyone. I think I can safely say Allie and I will always be firm friends.

We only had a couple of days left of our holiday, Allie had gone back home to Chicago, and Dawn was spending most of her precious time left with Mateo. I just wanted to chill, I wasn't looking forward to returning to work. Sam had stopped texting, I'm guessing that Jenny had finally had it out with him and let him know that she knew about us. I was pleased that he had stopped trying to contact me, I wasn't sure that I would be strong enough to resist him.

Chapter Fourteen

When I returned home the school wanted me to attend a teacher training course in Manchester, I wasn't sure exactly how to get there, so I decided to catch the train and then that way I wouldn't have to worry about finding it or parking. I walked to the station from home, I had purchased my ticket online and printed it out ready. I boarded the train at around 6.17 and searched the carriage for my reserved seat. 'Ah here it is, seat 44'. There was a nice big table for me to work at and looked like I was on my own - result.

I opened my laptop and logged in, only a few minutes later two men arrived. "Excuse me, could I just get into my seat please" A tall man stood to the side of me with his newspaper tucked neatly under his arm.

"Yes sure" I closed the lid of my laptop and squeezed out of my seat to let this rather posh bloke into his seat.

"Thank you"

"Welcome"

His companion sat opposite him, but they barely exchanged words apart from the odd comment about the news in the papers they were reading.

I really should have been looking at the day's agenda but I really couldn't be bothered. I sank back into my seat and lay my head against the red headrest. It would be a good couple of hours before I arrived in Manchester and I decided to rest my eyes for a few minutes. The next thing I know we are pulling into a station, I see a sign for 'Derby' as I smooth the palm of my hands over my face and look out of the window. I glance at the two very well to do gentlemen who are both still reading their newspapers. One had the daily telegraph and the other the daily express, neither of which would appeal to me. I stretch out after my forty winks and my feet touch someone else's. I look up and apologise. "Sorry" I look ahead of me, I am facing a rather hot guy.

"It's fine not a problem"

I feel an uncontrollable heat rushing across my face, and I am embarrassed at the thought of how red I probably look. He smiles, and I rapidly look down and prise open my laptop lid. I try to engross myself in my screen, reading my schedule for the day repeatedly. I want to steal another look at this guy that I am unexpectedly attracted to.

He's looking right at me; my eyes quickly focus back on to my laptop. I take yet another glance, his black-rimmed glasses give him a stimulating Clark Kent look, but an unshaven version.

"So where are you heading to?" He has a strong notable accent, but I couldn't distinguish where it was from, I bashfully replied.

"A training day with work, and you?"

"Same, well a business trip, what do you do?"

"I'm a teacher"

"Really!"

"You seem surprised"

He laughs and replies. "No, I'm not really, it's just I don't think I've ever met a teacher before"

"So, you didn't go to school?"

"Very dry, I think you know what I mean"

I smile back at him.

"What subject?"

"Sorry?" I found myself lost in him, so much so I hadn't heard what he had said.

"What subject do you teach?"

"Oh" I laugh awkwardly. "I teach English and Psychology"

"Interesting, what year?"

"Fifth and Sixth form. And what do you do?"

"I'm an IT manager"

"Oh? And what does that involve?"

"Do you fancy a coffee? And I'll fill you in on the boring stuff" he asked with a wink.

"Yes, thank you, that'd be lovely. I'll have a tea please"

"Sugar?"

"No thank you"

With that he wandered off down to the buffet carriage. I looked across at the gentlemen to my right, their papers were closed now, they didn't have a lot to say to each other. Perhaps they had made this journey every day and had run out of things to say. The man opposite had fallen asleep, the one next to me was staring out of the window. I'd say he was in his fifties, I glanced down at his hands - they were smooth and soft looking, he was obviously not a manual worker, I thought. I relaxed back into my seat and there he was again coming back towards me, two cups in hand.

"I assumed you wanted milk?"

"Oh yes, thank you" I said as I took my tea from him.

"So, where were we? Ah yes, my job. Well, in short, I advise organisation's and work out solutions that will enable them to perform more efficiently"

"I see, sounds..." I paused as I searched for the right way to say what I was thinking.

"Boring?" he laughed. "Yes, it is, but it's a job" He shrugged and took a sip of his drink.

We continued to chat and all too soon I had reached my destination. "Well this is me then"

He got up and shook my hand, a bit formal I thought but it was nice to feel his soft, firm hands. "Well nice to have met you, take care"

"Yes, and you" I grabbed my rucksack, threw my laptop into it and flung it over my shoulder. I made my way to the carriage door, and as I stepped off the train I looked back to give him a wave, but I couldn't see him. As the train pulled away I looked up to see if I could see him, but I couldn't, he was gone.

The rest of my day was, quite frankly, boring and I couldn't concentrate at all. All I could think about was him, the way I felt when I saw him and how he turned me on. I left the training session around five, my train wasn't due back to Leicester until 6:20pm so I decided to go for a bite to eat and a glass of wine. I found a little bistro near the railway station, settled down at a table for one and caught up with my social media. Time passed quickly and before I knew it, it was six o'clock and time to be boarding my train home. I swiftly gathered together my things and began to make my way to the station. It was at this point that I realised heels are not a clever idea when you must dash for something. I just arrived as the train pulled in. I checked my ticket to see where I was sat and figure out which coach to board - seat 44 again.

I made my way on to the train and to my seat. 'Yes, nobody there, just me' I'm wasn't in the mood for conversation. As I took my seat I noticed a briefcase was left on the seat opposite me, I guess I'm not alone after all, I thought. I placed my rucksack on the seat next to me and then heard a familiar voice come from above me.

"Well hello again"

My stomach does a summersault, it's him.

"So how did your day go?" He said as he sat down opposite me.

"Good, and you?" Suddenly I feel like talking.

"Oh, you know pretty much the same as any other day really. How about you, how was yours?"

"It was ok, well boring really, I hate training days"

"I know what you mean but you can put your training to effective use"

"Really, how?"

"Well any extra training can come in handy if you decide to further your career. Who knows, you might fancy teaching English abroad. Japan, China, Africa - the worlds your oyster" he said with a grin.

"I guess so, but it's not my thing really, I'm a bit of a home bird"

"It's good to spread your wings sometime, it doesn't have to be for good, just go and enjoy the experience"

"I know what you mean, but I don't think I could ever see me doing that"

"Well never say never"

I rest my elbow on the table and my head on my fist as I listen to him telling me to grab every bit of life, every minute, every moment. I find myself opening to him, telling him a bit about me, my loves and life, which didn't take long. He offered to buy me a drink again, but I insist on paying this time, after all he bought the first one. He jumped up and made his way to the buffet carriage, on his return I notice he's loosened his tie. I see he looks even hotter with that glimpse of flesh peeking through his shirt.

"Tea, no sugar"

He remembered, I don't think I would have. "Thanks" I reach into my rucksack for my purse, but he reaches over and holds my arm.

"No forget it, it's a cup of tea for heaven's sake"

We chat a while longer and I finish my tea, I'm about an hour from my destination and I don't want it to end. Then he leans over to me.

"I want you to go into the toilet, close the door but don't lock it"

I laugh as I say. "What?"

"You heard" he replied with a stern look on his face.

I remain seated, I look at the other passengers on the train, and turn back to look at him. "What if someone needs the loo?"

"They won't and if they do they'll just have to wait"

I laugh a little thinking he must be joking, but he raises his eyebrows back at me.

I smile nervously at him, he returns the smile and nods towards the toilet. "Look, I'm not really sure what -"

He presses his finger to my lips and signals to go to the toilet, I reach for my rucksack.

"It's fine, leave it here"

"But…"

No Rules

He laughs and says. "Just go"

Again, I look around the carriage then back at him, what sort of person does he think I am?

I lean towards him and whisper. "But you see, I'm not -"

He places his finger to his lips and looks directly at me. I notice how beautiful the hazel shade of his eyes is, his chestnut brown hair is cut short and swept slightly to the left side, mimicking the style of many hot young celebrities I've seen in magazines recently. I nervously smile at him, not believing that he can be serious but again he nods towards the toilet. I slowly stand and squeeze my way out of the seat.

I hesitantly make my way to the toilet; the motion of the train shifts me from side to side. I slide the door back and enter the toilet cubicle, pausing with my back against the closed door for a moment. I check myself in the mirror, check my teeth and hair, blowing my breath into my hands to check that it smells ok. I smooth my skirt down hoping it looks ok, though I'm not sure why as I realise it probably won't look like this for much longer. I feel apprehensive and wonder how long do I should wait? What am I waiting for? I'm beginning to feel nervous. Just as I'm about to leave, my hand reaching for the catch on the door, it slides open. I hesitate for a moment, startled, hoping it's him and no one else.

It was him.

He squeezed into the toilet with me and closed the door behind him, locking it. "Hi" He said in a low sexy voice.

"Hi"

He strokes the side of my face with the back of his hand, and gently sweeps the hair from the nape of my neck, then he kisses it. As he pulls away he lifts some of my hair in his hand and holds it up to his face, gently breathing it in. "I've been imagining this all day"

I pull back. "Have you?"

He puts his finger to my lips. "Shh, it got me through the day" His hand slides down to my hip and round to my bottom, squeezing it hard. I let out a gentle moan. His fingers search for the hem of my skirt, slowly moving it up he pulls it past the top of my stocking. He runs his finger along the top of it, stroking my naked flesh, pursuing my inner thigh. His hand moves up and slips into my pants, sliding into me with ease. I catch my breath as he enters me and gasp as his finger darts in and out.

He moans low in my ear, I reach for the zip of his neatly pressed trousers and release him. My hand hunts for his naked flesh, I wanted to touch him so bad, feel him against me. I grabbed the knot of his tie, pulling it free to reveal more of his chest. I open more of the buttons of his crisp white shirt. As I push the shirt over his shoulders he flicks the buttons on my blouse open, his flesh touches mine, soft and warm. Hitching my skirt further up he lifts me, resting me against the sink. He parts my legs; my shoes are set free from me and I rest my feet up against the wall opposite. He pulls my pants to one side and enters me. Oh, it's so good. We move in time with the gentle motion of the train. His hand moves around to my back and he unhooks my bra, his warm hand gently cups my breast as I gasp again. I glance in the mirror in front of me and for a second, I can't believe my reflection, I can't believe this is me.

Suddenly I begin to pant, feeling an orgasm building, the confined space of the toilet pulls us closer together. He kisses my breasts and I moan as he takes me deeper, his hands wrap around my bottom and he pulls me into him. My hands gently caress his back and then I am there. I stifle a moan as I bite into his shoulder. His pace quickens, and soon he was there with me. I tilt my head back, resting it against the wall of the train, letting out a sigh as I do it.

"We best be going, were nearly at your stop" He begins to fasten his shirt and secure his trousers.

"No, we have a while yet, don't we?" I reply as I tuck my blouse into my skirt.

He checks his watch. "No about five minutes I think"

I quickly pull myself together and fix my hair. I reach up to kiss him and he kisses me back. He winks at me as he fixes the top button of my blouse. "You leave first, and I will follow"

I nod back to him, it's like a precisely planned mission. I open the door slowly and wander back to my seat, filled with mixed emotions, embarrassment but also satisfaction. Just as I reach my seat we pull up to my station, I look towards the toilet door, but he doesn't appear. As I grab my jacket and rucksack I notice his briefcase is still on his seat. A moment later it's time for me to step off the train. My eyes search from the platform as I look to see if I can spot him, but again he's nowhere to be seen. I was sure he must have got on the train at the same time as me or just after.

As the train pulls away and leaves me standing alone on the platform I realise that I don't even know his name, or if I would ever see him again. I never spoke about him to anyone, not even my best friend Dawn. I don't know if I was embarrassed, or he was just my guilty secret, but either way I never mentioned my stranger on the train again.

Chapter Fifteen

The next day I had my lunch in the staff room, I still wasn't fully mixing with everyone there it wasn't really my style, but I thought it best to show my face every now and again. I sat on one of the couches at the back with a magazine, trying to ignore what was going on around me. Unfortunately, nobody seemed to want to give me some alone time, and Seb wandered over for a chat.

"So how was your holiday? I've not had chance to ask" He gestured to me to move up to let him sit down.

"Yes, it was good thanks, did you go anywhere?"

"No, well not really, I just went to visit some friends in Cornwall"

"That's cool, Cornwall is nice"

"Oh yeah, it was ok, we did a bit of surfing and that"

We chatted for a while, I hadn't spoken to Seb much since that night we spent together, only the odd passing conversation in the staff room.

"Listen I was wondering, do you fancy going for a drink sometime, just the two of us?"

This came a bit out of the blue, I wasn't expecting him to ask me out. "Yes, why not"

"Great! Shall we say Friday?"

"Yes, I think Friday should be ok"

"Great, we'll arrange a time nearer the end of the week"

I looked at my watch and realised I should be heading to my class. "Right I'll see you later then" I put my cup into the sink and headed to my class.

That evening as I was leaving work my phone bleeped with a text message. It was Paul, hmm I wonder what he wanted.

'Could we meet up sometime to tie up some loose ends?'

Loose ends? What an earth was he on about? I couldn't think of any loose ends left to tie up, but there was no harm in us having a chat. We are both adults and I'm sure we are sensible enough to talk anything through. I typed out my response and hit send.

'Yeah sure why not, when?'

To be fair we hadn't had much contact since the day he left, and I hoped it would clear the air between us. I arranged to meet him at a new bar on the high street called Harvey's, it was a rather cosmopolitan coffee house-cum-wine bar. I didn't want to meet anywhere that was familiar to us both, we had so many memories together.

The night we met up I arrived early, it was late September and it was still quite warm. It was a nice bar, quite modern looking. I ordered a white wine and found a seat near the window. Marvin Gaye was playing in the background, it was the perfect setting for a date, only this wasn't a date.

As I gazed out of the window I began to recall the memories Paul and I had shared together, my eyes began to glaze over. As I welled up with emotion I reached for a serviette on the table. I dabbed the corner of my eyes, taking care not to smudge my makeup. Just as I finished the door opened, it was Paul looking as lean as ever, his broad shoulders just fitting through the door frame. He smiled across at me, his perfect white teeth shining through his bronzed skin. He gestured across asking if I would like a drink. I held my full glass of wine up and shook my head. After a few minutes at the bar he came over and sat opposite me.

"So, how's things?"

"Good thank you, and you?"

"Yeah can't complain, busy with work etc, you know"

Yes, I did know, meeting new teachers, having a ball etc. I felt sick for a moment when I thought back to the time when I first caught him out. The smoothness of his voice suddenly snapped me out of my bitter thoughts and brought me back into the room.

"So, how's work with you?"

I looked across at him, tried to hate him, loath him, but it was no good I just couldn't do it. The butterflies in my tummy had already started dancing around. "Yes, it's good thank you, I love it at St Martin's"

"Good, good, have you made friends?"

I looked up at him and wanted to shoot his patronising question down in flames, but I didn't.

"Yes, thanks I've made friends, quite a few actually" One friendlier than the others I wanted to say, but I managed to refrain.

"That's good, and how's your Mum?"

'God this is ridiculous', I thought, he hasn't even been in touch with Mum since we separated, he was never that sort of guy. "Look I'm sorry Paul but what was it you were wanting to discuss? Loose ends I think you said"

"Yes, well just to see how you are really, you know catch up, that sort of thing"

I got up from the table and pushed the chair away with the back of my legs. "For God's sake Paul, I thought you wanted to sort something out!"

"I did... I do"

I brushed past and left the bar.

"Lizzie, wait!"

Tears rolling down my cheeks I walked as fast as I could.

"Lizzie, please!"

I could hear Paul sprinting towards me, he caught up and spun me around, pulling me off the main street into a doorway. By now I was crying, in fact sobbing. My eyes were tightly closed to try and shut this moment out of my life, I couldn't do this again.

"Lizzie, I'm sorry, truly sorry"

I looked up and as the street light lit his face up I could see he was also crying. I wiped away his tears with my thumbs. "I know Paul, I know you split with her, I bumped into Sarah from the offices"

"That was months ago when we split up. I couldn't stay with her, it's you I love, I always will. I could never love anyone like I love you" He held onto my arms, trying to pull me close to him.

"I can't do this, I need to go, let me go"

"Wait, let's just talk about it please" He held onto me tight, his hands clutching at my jacket.

I pushed past him and hailed a taxi.

"Lizzie please, I love you!" He pleaded with me as he stood with the taxi door open.

"Paul please close the door"

"No, not till you listen"

I can taste my salty tears as they fall and meet my lips. I close my eyes, hoping when I open them again he will be gone. With them still closed I say, "I can't right now, please just close the door"

"Five minutes that's all, we need to sort this out"

I leaned over to the taxi driver and asked him to drive away.

"I can't love, not till he closes the door" the driver replied, an apologetic but slightly annoyed look on his face.

I look back up at Paul still holding the door, begging me to get back out, and I yell wildly at him. "Paul just shut the fucking door!"

With a burst of anger, he slams the door shut. I sink back into the seat as the driver pulls away. I turn to look back to see Paul leant against the wall of the café, his hands in his pocket he looked like he had lost everything he had.

A few moments later I am back home, feeling totally drained. I hang my coat up and make my way upstairs to my once stress-free bedroom, where I had no problems to solve except for academic ones. But not tonight, no tonight it was filled with stress, down to a man named Paul.

I must have eventually got to sleep, but God knows what time, and the next day I woke with a blinding headache. I felt dreadful, worse than I would have if I had been out on the wine all night, which I resented as I had only had a sip. I laid in bed for a while wondering what he was playing at, why the sudden new-found interest in me.

I reached for my phone and turned it on, almost immediately it starts to bleep, there were six missed calls and four messages all from Paul.

'Please pick up I need to speak to you x'

'Just five minutes please x'

'Just hear me out x'

'Let me explain x'

I lay back on the bed holding my head in my hands and scream out loud. I glance at my bedside clock, seven forty-five, shit I needed to be at work. I quickly jump into the shower and skip breakfast, I wasn't that hungry anyway.

I wasn't myself at work, my head was a mess, why had he come back into my life? What did he want? I couldn't go through all that again. I join everyone in the staff room for mid-morning break. As I am pouring my coffee I hear Geoff ask, "Are you ok Lizzie?"
"Yeah, I'm good thank you, are you?"
"I'm ok, it's just you don't seem to be yourself today"
"Oh, I'm alright, I just didn't sleep that well last night"

"Well if you need anyone to talk to you know where I am" he smiled at me, patting my shoulder affectionately with his. Who would have thought Mr Bennett would be like that? I had read him all wrong.

"Thanks Geoff I appreciate that" I smiled back.

I continued through my day just going through the motions, trying to concentrate on the job in hand. Then mid-afternoon whilst I was taking class 6C there was a tap on my door. I looked up and it was Julie, I beckon her to come in. She leans over to me and whispers in my ear. "I'm sorry Lizzie, there's a call for you, said it was urgent"

I look up at her and suddenly felt a wave of sickness come over me. "Will you take my class please, it's all on power point"

"Sure, it's the phone in the deputy's office, there's no one in there"

"Thank you, I'll be back as quick as I can"

"Don't worry I can manage"

I felt like I had walked a mile to the office, my head was whirling, something must have happened to Mum. I hadn't been to see her for a while, oh God I hope she is ok. Or maybe it could be Dawn? After what felt like an eternity I finally reached the office and nervously picked up the phone, my heart was pounding like thunder.

"Hello?"

"Lizzie why haven't you been answering my text's? I've been ringing you too, you can't just dismiss me like this"

"Paul! I was worried sick! I thought it was Mum or Dawn, you can't ring me at work!"

Paul came back at me with an angry tone. "Well if you answered my call's I wouldn't have to!"

"I left my phone at home!"

"Look let's cut through all this red tape. I'll come to yours tonight and we'll have a chat, no distractions, we'll just sort it all out. I'll see you at eight"

I tried to say to him that there was no us. "But Paul, I really don't -" It was too late, he had already put the phone down. I sank into the chair in the office and began to cry, relief that the call wasn't from a member of my family but frustration that Paul was playing games. I grabbed a tissue from the box on the desk and held it against my red eyes.

"Miss Parks! Is everything ok?"

I look up and Miss Simmons the deputy head is stood in the doorway. I quickly wipe my eyes with the tissue. "Yes, I'm sorry, I just had to take a phone call"

"Not a good one by the looks of it?"

"Oh, its fine thank you, nothing I can't handle"

"Well even so, why don't you grab yourself a coffee and just have a few minutes in the staff room. Just to gather your thoughts"

"Yes, thank you, I think I will"

I made my way to the staff room and made myself a coffee. As I sat nursing the mug I began to cry again as I realised that no matter how much I try not to, I know I still love the man I have just spoken to.

Chapter Sixteen

I arrived home around six that evening, I was still churned up over the circumstances of the day so decided not to bother with any tea and just go straight up for a bath to see if I could relax my mind for a while. I turned the taps on and headed to the bedroom to try and find something to wear. I can't believe I'm letting Paul come around, although to be fair I wasn't, he didn't give me a choice.

I take practically everything out of my wardrobe and I can't find anything that I would feel good in, and then I see it, the lace dress I bought the day he walked out on me. I lay it out on the bed and wonder if it's too much, maybe I should just be casual and wear jeans. I make my way back to the bathroom to have a soak and think about it.

As I lay in the bath I try and make sense of the events of the day, I do still love Paul, I never stopped loving him. Maybe he does realise where he went wrong. I immerse myself into the water right up to my neck, then push my hands against the rim to help me climb out. Whichever way it goes I must find out why he wants to chat and what he wants to sort out. I dry myself off and wander into the bedroom and get myself ready.

It's seven thirty and I pour myself a large glass of wine, I have a feeling I am going to need it. My phone beeps, this will be him I thought, he will be cancelling. I check my phone to find that it's Caroline.

'I won't be home tonight I'm going to see a show with Jim. He's booked us into a hotel, so I will see you tomorrow evening x'

Lucky you I thought. I put some background music on at a reasonably low volume, took another large gulp of wine and curled up on the couch. As the time ticked by I recalled a time before when Paul was supposed to be coming home around seven. I fixed a nice meal for him, something I didn't do too often, and poured him a drink ready. But he didn't show, well not till eleven that evening, that was another time he spent with her and I dare say that's where he is now.

I picked up my empty glass and strolled into the kitchen to pour myself another, I felt a bit light headed but I hadn't really eaten all day. I poured another large measure and gulped it down. I filled the glass again and headed back towards the lounge. As I passed the mirror in the hallway I caught sight of my reflection. I placed my glass on the hall table and ran my fingers through my hair to give me a bit of a wild look, I piled it up on top of my head, I smiled, pouted and laughed at my image. Lipstick I thought, I haven't put any on. I searched around the drawer in the table until at last I found one. Red! Oh well it would have to do. I smeared it around my lips and pouted once again, I smiled and told myself. "You'll do"

I looked at my watch - it was eight twenty, oh well he wasn't going to come now. I went back into the lounge, kicked my heels off and settled onto the couch.

In the distance I could hear a knocking sound, I sat up and looked at my watch, it was eight forty-five, I must have fallen asleep. I jumped up, slipped my heels on and went to answer the door. There he was, filling the frame, white shirt, blue jeans and a suit jacket.

"Hi, sorry I'm late, I had to work extra, Bob rang in sick"
"No problem, come in, what would you like to drink?"
"I'll have a beer please"

No Rules

I stumbled into the kitchen, wow I needed to have some water, I had drunk way too much too quickly. I reached for a beer from the fridge for Paul. "Would you like a glass?"

"No, I'm fine thank you"

"Shall we sit through here?"

Paul followed me through into the lounge. I sat on the chair and he sat on the couch, there was an awkward silence in the room. I looked across at him and thought how I wanted to rip his shirt off and get him to fuck me. As his scent drifted over to me he smelt so sexy.

"So how have you been?"

At first, I didn't answer him, what could I say, 'I've been like shit since you left, nothings been the same and all I want now is for you to fuck me'. No, no I couldn't say that, I needed to play it cool. "Yes, I've been good really you know, holiday's, girly nights out, that sort of thing, and you?"

"Oh, not bad Suzanne and I split a few months back now, it could never have worked out, it's you I belong to"

I looked across at him and he looked back at me, filling my soul with his blue eyes. "You see I love -"

I get up from the chair and quickly interrupt him. "Would you like another drink?"

"Yes, why not" He holds his can up to me, I take it from him and make my way to the kitchen. I go to open the fridge and pause, what was I doing? I could feel my emotions building up in me, emotions I had spent the last few months trying to bury. Just then Paul called through. "So, how's the family?"

I open the fridge and grab another beer. "Ok, thank you" I call back as I pour myself another glass of wine. "Mum's still with Don, and Dawn well she's ok, still don't see enough of them all. How's your family?"

"Oh, they're all fine, thank you"

I step back into the lounge and sit next to Paul, he smiles as he takes the beer from me. We sit clutching our drinks. "You look beautiful Lizzie"

"Thank you" I choke back the tears as I tell him this was the dress I bought for him the day we were out shopping, the day he went to Suzanne's.

"I really am sorry Lizzie"

I press my finger against his lips, signalling him to be quiet. I didn't want this moment spoiling. He puts his beer on the small table by the couch, he turns to me and takes my glass of wine from me and places it next to his. As he turns back towards me we seem to be pulled together by an uncontrollable force that is somehow still between us.

He kisses me, and I instantly feel the rush he used to create in me. he traces his hand down my back, arousing me the way he always did. He caresses the nape of my neck with his lips, soft and warm and I find I am already wet for him. I slowly ease his jacket off and start to unbutton his shirt. As I slip my hand into it I feel his warm smooth chest, tanned, he was as sexy as ever.

"Oh Lizzie" He whispers in my ear.

I proceed to pull his shirt off whilst he begins to undo the zip on my dress, I stand up and turn around. He continues to unzip my dress and it falls to the floor, I'm not wearing a bra and my nipples stiffen from being exposed to the air. He kisses my shoulder as his strong hands stroke my breasts. I step out of my shoes and dress and undo his jeans before sliding my hand into his pants. He gasps as I hold him tightly, erect and ready for me. He pushes me down onto the couch, clutching at my pants he pulls them down.

I'm so ready for him, he spreads my legs and enters me so hard and with force. I scream out at the first thrust, his hands feel for my arse, clutching it he pulls himself into me again till we build up a familiar rhythm. Memories flood back of times before, I can feel the orgasm building up, he pulls out and I open my eyes to see why. He turns me round and enters me again. This time I'm there already, his hands move round and hold my breasts as he fuck's me like he never has before.

As my orgasm reaches its climax his does too, he lays on top of me and kisses my back as he traces patterns on it with his finger. I turn around to face him, he smiles at me as he says, "Does this mean we are back together?"

I smile back at him and I press my lips up against his, holding him tight. "I think it might do"

We lay together on the couch in silence for a while. I eventually move to look for my phone which had fallen to the floor in all the commotion, it was just after midnight and I had to be at work in the morning. I steadily roll off the side of the couch, I slip my dress back on and struggle to fasten it, I stand up and casually run my hands through my hair.

"Look I'm sorry to have to say but I have to be at work in the morning and it's gone twelve"

He pulled me back onto the couch. "Just five more minutes"

I started to giggle and pulled away from him. "Well as tempting as it is, I really can't I must be at work tomorrow"

"Ok, I get it, you've had me and now your throwing me out, I could always stay the night?"

I looked across at Paul and shook my head. "Not this time Paul"

After some time, I managed to persuade him to leave, he said he would ring me the next day.

Paul surprisingly stuck to his word and rang me at lunchtime the next day, he asked if I fancied going out that evening, but I declined. I didn't want to appear too keen. Instead we agreed to meet on Friday, once again I felt excited and happy that we were back together. I made my way back to the staff room to finish my lunch. Mr Bennett collared me.

"You seem brighter today Lizzie?"

"Do I?" I smiled back at him, knowing that I was probably happier than I had been in a long time. "Well yes I'm feeling pretty good thank you"

Mr Bennett smiled back and said. "Good I'm pleased for you"

As I left the staff room I bumped into Seb, literally. "Oh, Lizzie are we still good for Friday?"

I looked back at Seb. I had completely forgotten, Friday I said I would go out with him for a drink, well I couldn't go now, and I had to tell him why. "Ah, about Friday, I'm sorry but I won't be able to make it"

"No worries Lizzie, we can do it another time"

I looked back at Seb. "Well maybe not Seb, you see..."

Just then his phone rang. "Sorry I need to take this" He answered his phone and headed off down the corridor.

I didn't really get chance to say why I wasn't meeting up with Seb, but I doubt he would even think about it, he was after all a free spirit.

Over the next few weeks Paul and I were once again a couple, doing the same things we used to do. We soon fell into our old routine again. Then one night we were having a meal at mine and afterwards he called me over to sit on the couch next to him. I snuggled next to him, his left hand clasped my right hand, he looked deeply into my eyes and said. "Lizzie, I want to tell you something"

I smiled up at him. "You're not going to propose, are you?"

Paul looked back at me and smiled. "No, I'm not going to propose"

"Good because you would have to go some to beat our last wedding" Without taking a breath I proceeded to reminisce about our wedding while Paul just looked on.

"Lizzie, just stop, just for a minute"

I looked at Paul, he had a serious look, what was he going to tell me?

"Lizzie, I'm going back to Australia"

I stared back at Paul, I was shocked. He had done it again, hurt me. I pulled away from him and got up from the couch, he grabbed my hand again. "Wait let me finish"

"No, I've heard enough, what's the point?" I broke away from him and made my way into the kitchen.

Paul called through to me, I spun round and went back towards the lounge, Paul was coming towards me. "Lizzie, listen to me"

"Just go Paul" I walked towards the front door and opened it.

"But Lizzie, wait! Just listen to what I have to say"

I looked up at him. "I don't think there is anything else that you can say, just go"

"Wait I've got something else to say"

"I think you've already said enough, now go" I looked towards the floor trying to contain the tears that were trying to escape from my eyes.

Paul placed his hand on mine and closed the door. "Lizzie, listen to me for just one minute, you see, I want you to come with me"

I looked up at Paul and began to cry, it was me he wanted to be with, he was taking me with him.

The next few days were like a whirlwind, the time flew by, I gave my notice in and was surprised that so many of the staff were sorry to see me go. Julie was particularly upset, we had gotten quite close in the short time I was there, but I explained the circumstances and she was pleased for me. I promised her a night out and said I would arrange a leaving party. Seb wished me luck and said he looked forward to the leaving do. I wasn't even sure that he would turn up, but you never know.

Chapter Seventeen

The next person I had to let know, and the one I dreaded telling most, was Mum. This was one of the hardest things I have ever done, I just hoped she would understand and not be too disappointed in me for going so far away. I travelled down to see her that weekend, she was so pleased to see me, I felt so guilty having to tell her I was moving away. We sat and had a coffee and one of her delicious homemade scones.

"So, what brings you here then?"

I looked up at her. "What do you mean?" I said as I got back up to make myself another coffee, I could have done with something stronger if I'm honest.

"Well, I haven't seen you for a while so I'm assuming you have some news for me"

And indeed, I did have some news, if only she knew what.

"So, come on then, are you pregnant?"

I looked back at Mum in shock. "No, I am not pregnant!"

She started to laugh. "No, I didn't think so, I doubt I shall see that"

"Aww Mum, I'm not even sure I want kids, and Paul and I have just got back together. Give us chance!"

"I know Dear I'm only teasing. So, what is it then, money?"

"How do you know it's anything, I might have just come to see you"

Mum got up and came over to where I was standing and flicked the kettle switch on. "Look dear, I may be getting older, but you are my daughter and I happen to know you very well. I know when you need to tell me something and I think that is now"

I couldn't put it off any longer, I took a deep breath to prepare myself for what I was about to say. "Mum... Paul has asked me to go away with him"

"That's lovely news, where are you going? You deserve a holiday, you work so hard"

"It's Australia Mum"

"Australia! That's wonderful, what an opportunity. I've always fancied going there myself" She buzzed with excitement for me as she poured the freshly boiled water into her cup.

"Mum, it's not a holiday, it's to live"

As she reached for a teaspoon to stir her coffee the excitement fell from her face. "Oh, I see... well that's lovely news Dear" She continued to stir her coffee.

"Look, who knows Mum, it might not even work out. I mean we've already had one go at it"

"Oh, don't be silly Dear, I'm sure it will, and I'm so pleased for you. I'm glad you have sorted things with Paul, and although I will miss you I would never stand in your way. And who knows I might get out there to visit you sometime, if I live long enough to get there" She began to cry.

"Oh Mum" I held her tight and we cried together.

I spent the weekend at Mum's, Don left us to have some time together. We went shopping, out for lunch and watched some of our favourite movies. It was perfect and something we hadn't done for a long time, but it made my moving to Australia even more difficult. But I couldn't go back now, it was an opportunity I couldn't afford to miss.

After I left Mum's on the Sunday night I cried all the way home. I had never been too far from her, at least always in driving distance, but Australia was a lifetime away. I got home around 8pm and sat with a coffee reflecting on what I was about to do. This whole thing was going to be a life changing experience. But I would be spending it with Paul, and I loved him, didn't I?

I didn't sleep much that night, the weekend with Mum had made me think about what I was doing. The last thing I wanted to do was hurt her, but I knew that she understood why I had to do it and she wouldn't stand in my way, I was sure it would all work itself out.

The next day I arrived home from work around six thirty, I was feeling good and happy again. Paul and I were back together and this time we would make it. He'd said he would call me that evening to sort the final details out, and to be honest I couldn't wait. I had lots to look forward to. I had arranged to go on my works do the following Friday, and my head was filled with excitement.

Friday soon came and when I arrived at the bar in town the usual crowd were already there, Mr Bennett, Julie and a couple of others. I couldn't see Seb anywhere, he must have decided not to come. A little later I lined up the shots up for me and Julie, we had started how we meant to go on. When I had loosened up a bit I told Julie about my fears that were creeping in since I had been to see Mum, was I doing the right thing?

"Aww come on, everyone gets cold feet, you're going to Australia for Christ sake! What's not to like? I wish I was going, I'd love someone to whisk me off my feet. Let's face it there's not much to stay here for and if you don't like it you can always come home"

She was right I could and there would always be a job here for me. Paul had said I would soon get a job there though, I hope he was right.

Julie and I were just at the bar downing another line of shots, and bent double laughing, when I looked up to find Seb stood in front of me. He had a denim shirt on open at the neck, his hair looked like he had just run his fingers through it before he left his flat - to be fair that's all he needed to do - the curls fell in exactly the right places.

"Hi, you look like you're having fun"

I tried to compose myself.

"Can I get you ladies a drink?"

Julie quickly piped up. "I'm fine, I'll leave you guys to it"

Before I could ask her to stay she was gone. I leant against the bar in an effort to stay upright, Seb thrust a glass of wine in my hand.

"So, you're really leaving then?"

I looked back at Seb with a glazed expression, the after effects of too many shots with Julie, I took a sip of the wine he just bought me. "Yes, I'm definitely leaving"

"Well, I have to say I'll miss you"

I was surprised at his comment. "You hardly know me!"

Seb gently stroked my arm with his fingers. "Oh, I don't know... I think I know you pretty well" He leaned forward and pressed his lips against mine, I began to respond, and he pulled away. "Oh, I maybe shouldn't have done that, sorry. After all you're not free and single anymore"

I wrapped my fingers round his neck and pulled him towards me. We locked together tightly, it felt so right, then suddenly we were interrupted by Julie.

"Sorry to interrupt guy's but we are thinking of moving on, are you coming?"

Seb and I quickly pulled apart, and I replied. "Yes of course we are, where are we going?"

"There's a bar a bit further along, can't remember the name but it's the next one"

"Cool we will be there in a few minutes, we'll just finish these drinks"

Julie gave me a kiss on the cheek and whispered. "I bet you don't come"

I whispered back. "I will I promise"

"Ok, see you soon"

I watched Julie disappear through the crowded bar, I grabbed my wine and Seb bent forward and said. "We could slip away and go back to mine?"

I looked up at him smiling and replied. "And that's not a good idea at all"

"Why not? I think it's an excellent idea"

I shook my head.

Seb laughed. "Is it the stairs putting you off? I'll carry you"

I started to laugh. "No, it's not the stairs. Come on drink up, we'll catch them up" I grabbed Seb's hand and we pushed our way through the crowded bar.

As we reached the street it was pouring with rain, Seb pulled me into a door way and tried again to persuade me to go back to his.

"No come on this is my leaving do, I have to be there"

We ran through the rain to the next bar, when we got in Seb spotted everyone sat in the corner. I made my way over to them whilst Seb headed to the bar.

Julie looked surprised to see me. "Lizzie, you made it!"

"Of course, told you I'd be here" I smiled back at her.

Seb was soon back with the drinks, we all settled in when Julie spoke up that she needed the loo. "Are you coming to the loo with me Lizzie?"

"No, I'm ok thanks"

"I need a word" Julie replied and winked at me.

I got up and followed her, as soon as we got in she turned to me and asked. "So, are you going back to Seb's for a farewell shag"

I looked at myself in the mirror, I looked like I had just got out of the shower. I reached for a paper towel and tried to dry my hair. "Julie! What do you mean?"

"Aww come on, I would have said it's a dead cert"

"Well you would be wrong. I have no intension of going back to his"

"So, he's asked you then?"

"No, well maybe… Well ok yes, he has, but I said no"

"But you will go"

I closed my eyes and knew she was right, I was tempted, but I couldn't, in fact shouldn't go. I applied some lipstick and some blusher in an attempt to rid myself of the washed-out look, I called out to Julie. "Come on what are you doing in there"

"I'm trying to sober up"

"Oh, I don't feel so bad now, I think the rain sobered me up"

Just then Julie came out of the toilet. "So, is it raining?"

"No, I always come out with wet hair" We both started to laugh.

We headed back to the table and soon fitted back into the conversation. It wasn't long before we moved to the next bar, and the drinks were flowing well. Later that evening we were down to the four of us again, me, Julie, Geoff and of course - Seb. We all sat and chatted about how badly done to us teachers were and the politics behind teaching, and then Seb said. "Anyway, Lizzie won't have to worry about that soon, when she moves to Australia. Have you got a job out there?"

"Well not exactly, but Paul assures me that I will be able to get one easily enough"

Julie reached for her glass and said. "Well it's a bit late to worry about that now"

Geoff quickly replied. "Oh, I wouldn't worry I'm sure there will be plenty of work out there for you Lizzie"

Julie picked up his comment. "Well I was always under the impression that you had to have a job lined up before you went out to Australia"

I looked across at her, why was she being like this, her mood had changed, I stood up from my chair. "Look I'm going to get off, I've still got a lot to do so I'll be up early in the morning. Thank you all for coming it's been great, I'll see you all on Monday"

I spun round and made my way out of the bar, I could hear Seb calling to me in the distance. "Lizzie, wait!"

He finally caught up with me. "Look come back to mine, just for a drink, coffee if you want? Just don't go like this I know she's upset you"

I quickly wiped a tear from my cheek. "No, I'm fine, I best not"

Seb put his arm around my shoulder. "Come on, we'll just chill out, just me and you. We haven't chatted for ages"

We walked up to the taxi rank and before I knew it we were on our way. We travelled to Seb's in silence, he held my hand in the back of the taxi, I could feel him staring at me. I glanced his way.

"Hey, are you ok?"

"Yes Seb, I'm fine thank you" I smiled back at him trying to hide the torment that was happening in my head.

Chapter Eighteen

We pulled up outside Seb's. I was feeling quite sober now, the bulk of the alcohol had worn off during the journey. Seb paid for the taxi and we made our way up the many stairs to his room. When we got inside things were pretty much the same as they were last time, a small table lamp lit the room. A pile of dishes sat in the sink, and an unkempt rug sat in the middle of the floor.

"So, what's it to be, tea, coffee or wine?" He looked back at me with a cheeky grin and a bottle of chardonnay in his hand.

I smiled back at him and said. "I think you already know the answer"

He picked up a tumbler from the sink, gave it a quick swill and half dried it before he poured me a very large wine. I took the glass from him and drank a large mouthful of it. He nodded at me to move up on the couch and sat next to me. "So, what's with you and Julie this evening?"

"Oh, I don't know. We usually get on really well, but she just suddenly started going on about me moving away"

"Maybe she's jealous, or more to the point she's going to miss you"

"Well she has a funny way of showing it" I snapped back at him.

"I wouldn't take it too much to heart, she will have probably forgotten about it once the alcohol has worn off in the morning"

I had another drink of my wine and began to tell Seb about how I felt, and how uncertain I was about everything.

"You just need to relax Lizzie, and I think I know what you need" Seb leaned forward and kissed me. I wanted to resist and stop this ache for him building up inside me, but I couldn't. I kissed him back, pushing him hard against the sofa. Threading my fingers through the curls in his hair, pressing my lips against his brow taking the scent of him in. For a second, I felt I couldn't breathe, I wanted him so much. I paused to take a breath.

"I think some ones missed me" Seb whispered seductively.

I moved myself to sit astride him and pulled at the press studs on his denim shirt, revealing his chest, which was nothing like Pauls. No muscles to be seen and certainly no tan. Just Sebastian, hot looking Seb, the man who practically taught me the Karma Sutra in one night.

I gently kissed his chest, my hands searching for the zip on his jeans. I began to slide his zip down slowly, pushing my hands into his jeans. He swept my hair aside before he kissed my neck, he sent a shiver through me as he did, and I was wet at the thought of him. He spun me around on the couch and yanked at my pants trying to pull them down, I lifted my bottom trying to help him. He kissed me again. I kissed him back as I pushed the waist of his jeans down.

I lay there, my legs spread wide waiting for him, I pulled him close as he entered me. I screamed out with satisfaction, he built up speed and I began to fill with pleasure, crying out as I reached my climax.

Shortly after he followed slumping on top of me as he climaxed. I went to the bathroom to clean myself up, when I came out he was nowhere to be seen, his bedroom door was open slightly.

"I'm in here, come join me" he shouted through.

I wandered over into the bedroom, he was snuggled under his quilt.

"Look I'm just going to get dressed and head off"

"Don't be silly, stay here the night" He flicked the quilt back and patted the bed for me to join him.

I walked over and sat on the edge. "I don't know, it might be best if I just get off and go home"

"It would be best if you stay here and go home in the morning. Trust me, you don't want to be going at this time, there'll be no taxi's available" He bent forward and kissed me and suddenly we were locked together again. I don't know what it was, but he had something that drew me to him, like a moth to a light. Something that I really shouldn't touch, as I knew I would get burnt, but I still did it. I curled into him and after no time at all drifted over to sleep.

When I woke up we were still locked together, I checked my watch it was nearly five thirty. I looked up at the sky light and the stars filled it like a framed picture, sparkling like diamonds. It may sound like a cliché, but it really was an amazing view. I thought about Paul and how hurt he would be if he knew what I was doing. To be honest my head was so fucked up now I didn't know what I was doing. I had to get out of here, I didn't want to be here in the morning, making an embarrassing exit like I did last time.

I left the room as quietly as I could and gathered my clothes from the living room. I went to the bathroom, got myself dressed and tried to make myself presentable for the outside world. When I got outside it was just beginning to get light, I decided to walk home or at least until I could flag a taxi down. I needed to clear my head and sort this mess out.

I got home around 7am, and went straight up to bed, but I struggled to get to sleep, my head was all over. After a couple of hours of questioning my actions the night before I managed to drift off to sleep. I can't have been asleep long before my phone rang. It was Paul. I wasn't sure I could speak to him right now, so I pressed to silence the ringtone and ignored it. I pulled the quilt over my head hoping this mess would go away. A few minutes later my phone rang again, it was Paul again. The mess hadn't gone away, I had to answer.

"Hi"

"Good morning, I'm guessing you are still in bed? I've been trying to ring you"

"Oh, sorry yes I was asleep"

"You had a heavy night then?"

I felt the guilt well up inside me again, if only he knew. "Yes, you could say that"

"What time did you get in?"

"I can't remember, it was late though" Possibly two or three hours ago I thought.

"Oh well as long as you enjoyed it. Listen I thought I could come to yours this evening and we can sort out all the fine details? Did I tell you I've got a job and there's another post at the same school, it sounds perfect and…"

"Paul slowdown" I had to interrupt, I couldn't think straight. "Yes, you come to mine tonight Paul and we'll have a chat about it all"

"Ok, I will, are you excited Lizzie?"

I paused, I wasn't excited, I wasn't anything, just numb"

"Lizzie are you there?"

"Sorry yes I think the signal went a bit I couldn't hear you. What did you say?"

"Nothing its ok we'll talk later; shall we say eight?"

"Ok, see you tonight" I ended the call and threw my phone on the bed. I held my head in my hands and pulled at my hair, what had I done and what was I doing? The truth was I didn't know. Did I really want to go down the same road I had been down before? How could Paul even think that I would want to work in the same school as him after the last time? Everything was a mess, a real mess.

I ran myself a hot bubble bath and immersed myself into it. No book this time, just me and my thoughts. My head was still spinning, wondering what to do. I could feel myself drifting off to sleep so I decided to go back to bed to catch up for a bit longer. No matter how long I thought about last night I couldn't change anything now. I crawled back in and snuggled under the duvet, closed my eyes and drifted off to sleep.

I woke up about five, much later than I had planned. I think the pressure of the last few days had caught up with me, there is a lot to do when you are moving abroad. I got myself dressed and made my way down to the kitchen, opened the fridge but I couldn't see anything that I fancied, it wasn't a secret that I hated cooking for myself. I found some ham, it was open but still smelt ok. I made myself a sandwich and opened a bottle of wine pouring myself a glass.

Paul was early, I opened the door and he kissed me on the cheek as I let him in. "Hi, do you want a beer?"

"Sure"

I brought a beer from the fridge. Paul was already settled on the couch, so I went over and sat next to him. He began to go through all the plans for the big move, I sipped my wine and tried to listen with interest as he told me what would be happening after we arrived in Australia and where we would be living. I found my thoughts wandering to the events of last night and the previous months that I had been separated from Paul. Just then I was brought back into the room as Paul repeated my name.

"Lizzie are you listening?"

"Yes of course I am"

A little later I asked Paul if we could change the subject for a while.

"But aren't you excited Lizzie?"

"Yes, I'm excited but can't we just relax a bit"

I leant forward and kissed him, slipping my fingers into his open shirt running my hand over his chest. He kissed me back, his lips were wet and soft, I could taste the beer on them. I started to unbutton his shirt. I peeled it back and revealed the muscles I was so familiar with, this was what I ached for, I had wanted him back for so long, I had craved for this moment since the day he walked out on me. I loved him, didn't I?

My head was beginning to spin again, I pushed these ridiculous doubts from my mind and focussed on the man I was about to spend the rest of my life with. He knelt in front of me, as he kissed my neck he reached for the buttons on my blouse, hurriedly unbuttoning them. I felt his soft lips kissing between my breast. He pulled my bra down and as his lips kissed me I could feel my desire for him heighten. He slowly traced his tongue along my body until he reached the place I had been waiting for.

His tongue darted deep within me and a deep sensation rose within me. A hot feeling, a tingle and numbness all at once, an explosion of pleasure. As I came he undid he jeans and entered me, he was ready, so firm and hard. I cried out as he pushed deep inside me and fucked me like never before. As he lay on top of me afterwards I stroked his hair and wondered what our future together would hold.

The next day Paul went home, and I decided to pack my case. I hadn't thought about what I needed to take, I was just going to pack a few things to begin with and see what else I would need when I got there rather than take a lot of stuff I wouldn't need. Mum had said she would organise to have some things shipped out to me when I was settled, and she said I could store my things there till a later date.

I went into work on the Monday earlier than usual. I was nervous about going, I wasn't sure how Julie or Seb would be with me. I bumped into Julie first and luckily, she was fine, she came up to me in the staff room and admitted that she was in fact going to miss me. She said she hadn't really got on this well with anyone in the school, and she doubted that she would again. I gave her a hug and said that she must come and visit and that I would stay in touch via social media, email etc. Then she asked me the question I was dreading.

"So, did you end up at Seb's?"

I looked back at her and nodded. "I knew you would, was it a goodbye shag?"

"No, it was... Oh, to be honest I don't know what it was, but it should never have happened"

"Funny, you said that last time" We both began to laugh, just as we did the door to the staff room opened and in he walked.

"I'll see you later Lizzie, I've got some prepping to do for my class, besides I think someone might want a chat with you"

I grabbed my coffee and stepped forward to move away from the work surface. Seb intercepted my move and stood in front of me. "So, what's up then don't you like my coffee?"

I looked up and him and smiled uneasily. "What do you mean?"

"Well no one's ever ran out on me before at least having a coffee"

"I had lots to do, and I was afraid I would lie in"
"Oh, so you are going through with it then?"
"What do you mean?"
"Well the other night you couldn't decide if you wanted to or not"
If I had been honest with myself I still wasn't sure. "I think that was last minute nerves. It's a long way and life changing, but exciting too"
I don't know who I was trying to convince.
"Yes, you said all that the other night too, but as long as you are sure that's all that matters"
And that was just it I wasn't sure about anything anymore.
The day went quickly, as did the week, in fact the following two weeks passed quicker than I wanted. I had my last day at work, which was very emotional. We had a farewell buffet and I promised to stay in touch with everyone. Everything seemed to be moving so fast, Paul was bombarding me with schedules, times and things we had to do. Safe to say I was feeling overwhelmed.
A few days before we were due to fly Paul rang and said that he had to go to London, something to do with his new job, he was hoping I would go with him.
"There's no way I can come with you!"
"Why not? We can take in the sights and relax before we fly"
"Absolutely not, I have way too much to do"
"Like what?"
I could feel this escalating into an argument which I didn't need right now. "Look I seriously have too much to do at the moment. I'm just going to have to meet you at the airport"
"I just thought it would give us chance to relax"
"Sorry Paul but I can't, I really have too much to do"
"Ok, I'll see you there then"
With that he put the phone down. I'm sure he would get over it and I was too busy to fret over him now.
The next day Paul left for London, he came around in the morning to see me. "I'm sorry about yesterday I was just trying to give us some time to relax before that long flight"

"I know you were, and I appreciate it, but I really do have some lose ends to tie up. I want to spend some time with Caroline, she's been good to me"

"I know, and I understand" He kissed my forehead and whispered. "I love you"

"I know, I'll see you on Friday" I kissed him and held him tight, we broke away and I watched as he made his way down the path to his waiting taxi.

I really needed to get things together now and get sorted for Friday, this was really one of my downfalls. I had no organisational skills, I can still hear my teacher saying it to me now, how the hell I became a teacher I will never know.

Before I knew it, Thursday was here and in less than twenty-four hours my life would be changing, and now I couldn't wait. That night I thought I would treat Caroline to tea, nothing fancy just a chilli, it would save her when she gets in. Let's be honest she had made mine often enough.

I tried to take my time as I wanted it to be right, she would be home at seven thirty after her gym session. Caroline actually got in around seven, earlier than I expected. She went up for a shower and I popped the garlic bread in the oven. When she came down I had set everything out for her, there was a large bowl of chilli in the middle of the table and a tray of garlic bread.

"This looks nice, what's the occasion?"

"It's my leaving meal from me to you"

Caroline came over and gave me a big hug. "Aww bless you" She took a seat at the table. "So, are you all ready to go?"

"Kind of, well I think so" Paul had called me today, and things couldn't have been better.

"Well I wish someone would take me to Australia"

I was shocked by Caroline's comment, I always thought of her as more of a home bird. Come to think of it I thought I was but here I am about to leave to move to the other side of the world!

"Really? I wouldn't have thought it was your thing"

"No, it's not really, I just fancy a bit of an adventure"

"What sort of adventure are you looking for?"

We both started to laugh, I reached over to the fridge to get another bottle of wine. As I poured us another glass I asked her again. "So, come on what sort of excitement are you looking for?"

"Well I don't think I will ever have the sort of excitement you have had in your life the last few months"

I felt myself blush a little and hid my face with my wine glass. "Well it's been colourful I'll say that"

"Yes, it has" Caroline got up and started to walk around the kitchen with her wine.

"Well let's see there's been a school teacher, a married man, a lesbian fling and Paul again. And they are only the ones I know about"

I began to laugh. "God you make me sound awful!"

"No, you're not awful, you've just enjoyed yourself which is what life is all about"

I wasn't sure my mum would have seen it like that, or Paul for that matter, but yes Caroline was right I had just had a little fling I guess and let my hair down a bit.

We stayed up until the early hours drinking wine, laughing and reminiscing about times when we were younger and before we grew apart. That seemed to happen when we met our partners and then I married Paul and we seemed to drift further away from each other. When I split from Paul Caroline was there to help me. But we were different people when I moved in with her, we had different ways of doing things. For starters Caroline was super healthy, and I wasn't. This time with Caroline was like old times and the best we had had for a long time, I was going to miss her.

I got up the next day around nine with a bit of a sore head, Caroline had already left for work. I made myself a coffee and pulled myself round, I had to get to the airport for about twelve, we were due to fly at three.

I gathered my bags together and had one last look round before I left, I couldn't complain Caroline had been good to me. As I waited by the door for my taxi my phone beeped - it was Paul.

'Not long now, hope you are on your way'

I didn't have time to reply as my taxi had just pulled up.

I arrived at the airport and checked in, the part I hated most of all. I travelled up the escalator to the next floor, when I arrived at the top my phone bleeped again.

'Are you here yet? I can't see you anywhere'

I made my way to the other side of the airport, dragging my hand luggage with me. I settled down at a table in the first café I came to and ordered a cappuccino. Once again, I thought about what I was about to do. An hour went by as I reflected on what had been happening in the last few weeks, meeting up with Paul again and thinking about what lie ahead. My phone beeped once again, it was another text from Paul.

'Where are you?'

I stared at my phone not able to reply. I looked around the airport, taking in the people around me wondering where their planes were about to take them and what adventures they had in store. I was startled by an announcement.

'Would all passengers for flight NoVA491 departing for Australia please board now'

My phone bleeped again, it was Paul.

'We must board now'

'Come on Lizzie, where are you?'

A tear escaped from my eyes, just one that's all, there would be no more. Not for Paul anyway. I stared down at the plane ticket I was holding bound for Hong Kong. Who knows what lay ahead, new sights, new adventures… maybe a new relationship, we will have to see. I brushed the tear away and made my way to the gate. I just made it and was hurried along to board the plane. I walked up the large stairway of the aircraft. and showed my ticket to the hostess.

"25b Madam, half way down on the left"

I made my way further down the plane and I could see him, dark hair and unshaven, his hazel eyes mesmerizing me the way they did before.

"Excuse me, do you mind if I sit here?"

He gave me a familiar smile and replied. "Sure, be my guest"

I sat myself next to him and secured my seat belt.

"That was lucky" he said.

"What was?"

"Well, that you text me"

I looked back at him and replied. "No, it was lucky that your business card fell into my bag"

"Really?!"

I looked up at the stewardess about to perform her flight safety demonstration and whispered back to him. "Yes really"

"And did it really fall in your bag?"

I glanced back at him and he tried to suppress his laughter. As the plane accelerated on the runway and the wheels left the tarmac I looked out of the window wondering what lay ahead. And as for my companion, my stranger on the train, well he was here and that's all that mattered.

He leaned into me and said. "In a few minutes go to the bathroom, don't lock the door and wait for me"

I turned and laughed at him, this was going to be some ride, and who knows how long it would last. But to be honest, right now, I didn't care.

Printed in Poland
by Amazon Fulfillment
Poland Sp. z o.o., Wrocław